REFLECT YOU ARE AWESOME!

this **novelzine™** is the property of:

name: _____

God Wants You to Shine

It's okay to be down once in a while.

But even in those times, God wants you to smile.

It may hurt, and it may not feel good.

But in your down time,

remember the cross where Jesus stood.

He stood steadfast for you.

He bled and died 'cause His love is true.

And even though things right now

don't seem fine,

God wants you to rely on Him.

God wants you to shine.

All Scriptures are quoted from the HOLY BIBLE, NEW INTERNATIONAL VERSION®. NIV®. Copyright© 1973, 1978, 1984 by the International Bible Society. Used by permission of Zondervan. All rights reserved.

Cover by Koechel Peterson and Associates, Inc., Minneapolis, Minnesota

Interior design by Koechel Peterson and Associates, Inc., Minneapolis, Minnesota

NOVELZINE is a trademark of The Hawkins Children's LLC. Harvest House Publishers, Inc., is the exclusive licensee of the trademark NOVELZINE.

AUTHOR: Stephanie Perry Moore
MANAGING EDITORS: Carolyn McCready and Terry Glaspey
PROJECT MANAGERS: Betty Fletcher and LaRae Weikert
PROJECT EDITOR: Hope Lyda
EDITORIAL REVIEW: Penny Bell, Michele Clark Jenkins, and Brenda Noel
FAITH CHARACTER: Nicole Bell
OTHER CHARACTERS: Chris Bell (Dad), Macy Bell (Belle), Penny Bell (Mom), Taylor Bell (Joy), Lindsey Kilpatrick (Nellie), Brenique Lewis (Holly), Brianna Lewis (Hope), Shelby McClure (Kendal), Jacob Lewis (Niles), and Hunter Phillips (Blake)
PHOTOGRAPHY: Bonnie Rebholz [www.bonnierebholz.com]
STYLIST: Amy Baumann
WARDROBE: Rave Girl
MAKEUP AND HAIR: Kim Barclay
AUTHOR'S ASSISTANTS: Jessica Phillips, Ciara Roundtree, and Ashunda Moon
FEATURES AND ARTICLE WRITERS: Penny Bell, Michele Clark Jenkins, Stephanie Perry Moore, Jessica Phillips, and Brenda Noel
AUTHOR SPECIAL THANKS TO: Mel Banks Jr., Derrick Moore, Sydni Moore, Sheldyn Moore, Cynthia Ballenger, DeeAnn Grand, Dana Long, Marjorie Kimbrough, Selena James, Shirley Perry, Franklin Perry, Sarah Lundy, Andrea Johnson, Torian Colon, Robin Jones Gunn, Jenell Clark, Jackie Dixon, Tawainna Brown-Bolds, Tabatha Palmer, Deborah Bradley, Joy Nixon, Vanessa Davis Griggs, Bob Sanford, Leon Thomas, and Laurie Whaley

GOD WANTS YOU TO SHINE
Copyright © 2007 by Stephanie Perry Moore

Published by Harvest House Publishers
Eugene, Oregon 97402

www.harvesthousepublishers.com

Library of Congress Cataloging-in-Publication Data

Moore, Stephanie Perry.
  God wants you to shine / by Stephanie Perry Moore.
    p. cm. – (Faith Thomas series) (Novelzine ; #2)
  Issued in a magazine format with sidebars, photographs, and callouts.
  Summary: Fourteen-year-old Faith Thomas, the daughter of a popular Christian musician, learns to trust God as she struggles with friendship problems, her feelings for boys, and the pressures of a beauty pageant.
  ISBN-13: 978-0-7369-1920-3 (pbk.)
  ISBN-10: 0-7369-1920-1 (pbk.)
  [1. Christian life–Fiction. 2. Friendship–Fiction. 3. Beauty contests–Fiction.] I. Title.
  PZ7.M788125Gnu 2007
  [Fic]–dc22
                            2007001825

All rights reserved. No part of this publication may be reproduced, stored in a retrieval system, or transmitted in any form or by any means—electronic, mechanical, digital, photocopy, recording, or any other—except for brief quotations in printed reviews, without the prior permission of the publisher.

Printed in China

07 08 09 10 11 12 13 14 15 / RDS / 10 9 8 7 6 5 4 3 2 1

God Wants You to Shine

by Stephanie Perry Moore

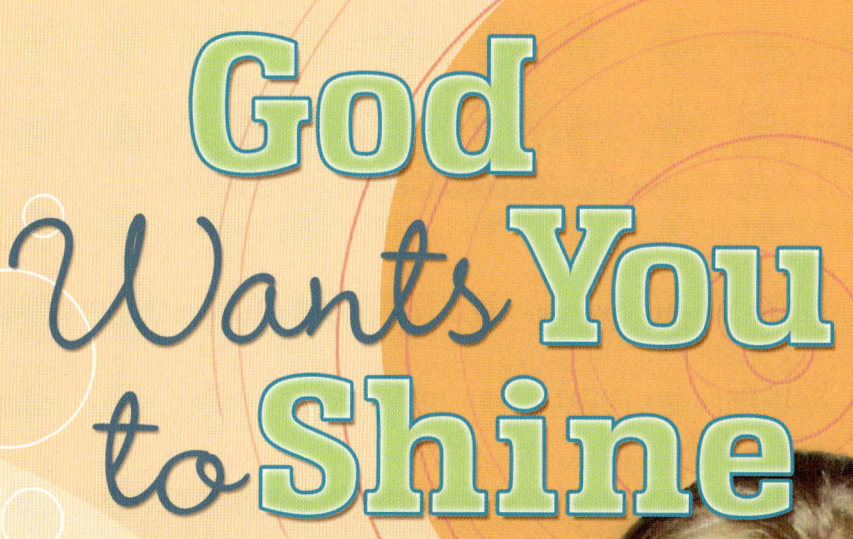

HARVEST HOUSE PUBLISHERS
EUGENE, OREGON

[special features]

›› **Self-Esteem Grows**............23, 49, 71, 91, 113, 133

›› **Self-Esteem Quiz: Poise or Poison?**.............72

[articles]

›› **Scrapbooking 101**...................140

›› **The Third Person**...................141

›› **Gettin' Quiet**.....................141

›› **About the Model**...................142

›› **About the Author**..................143

›› **Sounds 2 ✓ Out**...................144

[contents]

CHAPTER

1. ›› Pictured Things Better.....................6
2. ›› Jumbled Up Inside..........................18
3. ›› Focused on Him.............................30
4. ›› Lacked the Confidence....................40
5. ›› Hoped for Change..........................52
6. ›› Stressed-Out Completely.................62
7. ›› Surprised by Confidence..................74
8. ›› Ended the Misery...........................86
9. ›› Renewed My Beliefs.......................98
10. ›› Betrayed but Positive....................108
11. ›› Beamed with Pride........................118
12. ›› Shined So Bright..........................128

CHAPTER 1:

january

Pictured Things Better

Have you ever wondered why things go wrong? Like no matter what you do to make stuff right, something or someone messes up your great plans? If so, I understand. I'm so sick of my days having drama. Can't one day just be perfect? Well, read along and see if my life gets straightened out.

Can't one day just be perfect?

[CHAPTER 1]
Pictured *Things* Better

I sat on my bed staring out the window at the backyard. It was such a beautiful day outside. The sun was shining, and evidence of God's creative touch was everywhere. I happily started to daydream, and then I heard my friend Nellie's voice bellowing through the telephone. Her tone alone brought me back to the conversation with a jolt.

"So you know you can't date my brother, right?" Nellie stated matter-of-factly, yet I would've sworn she had practiced it.

I couldn't believe what I was hearing. I looked at the picture on my nightstand of Nellie and me. I wanted to toss it across the room. Here she was, my best friend, a person I had depended on to encourage me in my faith last year...and she didn't think I was good enough to date her brother? She only recently found out that the guy I was sort of crushing on *was* her brother, but I never said I wanted to date Niles. And if I did want to, who was *she* to tell me I couldn't? Especially since she thought it was all sort of cute and funny that her brother was the mystery man I had mentioned.

"Faith, are you there? Hello!" Nellie barked into the phone rudely.

"Quit biting my head off. I'm here," I retorted.

"I don't want to hurt your feelings, but I'm not comfortable with the thought of you and Niles together. So before anything starts, I figured I'd set the ground rules."

"Who are you to decide?" I asked her abruptly as I sat up straight. "Nellie, I don't want to argue with you, so let's just hang up for now."

"No. I'm not going to hang up."

"You're acting like I'm in love with Niles. I don't even know how I feel."

"Obviously you feel something, or it wouldn't matter that I'm taking him off the table."

"Look, Nellie, at church last week you acted like it was great Niles and I were talking to each other. So why this change of heart? If you get right down to it, what should it matter? If you're truly my friend, you'll respect my decisions."

> "You're acting like I'm **in love** with Niles. I don't even **know** how I **feel**."

"You should be thanking your lucky stars that I'm telling you not to date him. It's more for your benefit."

"Why? Does he like a lot of girls? Is he a total dog or something?"

"He's just full of himself." Nellie seemed to stall for a moment. "He's not the kind of boy who would know how to consider your heart. You get what I'm saying?"

Not exactly. I stared at that photo of Nellie and me again. What was up with her?

"You're being quiet. That means you're either ticked or confused. Let me make this clear and simple. You're friends with me. And you'd like to be friends or more with Niles. You can't be loyal to both of us, so think on it and call me back later."

Her voice ended and a dial tone started. I stood there amazed, holding the receiver. I got up and went into my bathroom. I stared at my reflection. Blah. I felt and looked blah, bland, pasty white, invisible. I played with my hair, but I wished it had more spunk. I grinned and looked at my teeth. I wished my braces were off. I patted my cheeks to give them some color. It was useless.

"Why am I not satisfied with me?" I said to myself. Everybody thought I looked cute. I could hear my friend Hope's voice in the back of my mind telling me I had it going on, but she was the one with pretty mocha skin that practically glowed.

I desperately needed the sun. As nice as today was, this was still Tennessee in winter. Too bad my family didn't plan winter vacations in Hawaii like a lot of other families in the neighborhood. Maybe my mom would let me go tanning at her fancy gym. In the past she had always said, "No, you're great just the way you are." Parents. I swear they have ten favorite lines they use to address anything a teen says. They probably go to online chat rooms and exchange their boring lines for other lame lines.

BEHIND THE SCENES
ON FAITH

FULL NAME: Faith Noel Thomas
BIRTH DATE: December 25
FAMILY MAKEUP: Dad, Mom, younger sister, Joy, younger brother, Blake
FAVORITE COLOR: Tangerine (this year)
FAVORITE FOOD: Pizza
HOBBIES: Scrapbooking and cheerleading
GOALS: Longs to believe in herself.
STRENGTHS: Loves to find the best in people.
WEAKNESS: Can't find the best in herself.
ONE POSITIVE ABOUT THIS CHARACTER: Though she struggles, she seeks to find ways to make her life better.
WORD OF INFLUENCE: Grow
FAVORITE PHRASE: Life is what you make it, so make it good.

But now I was in high school. I was a ninth grader, dang it, and I needed some pizzazz in my life. Mom had already agreed to let me wear a little makeup. Maybe changing my skin color with the assistance of technology was a request she would finally grant. I could always play up the "other kids get to go to Hawaii" angle.

> So **why** do we still question our **value** and our **beauty** so much?

I looked out of my bathroom door and saw my mom passing by.

"Mom!" I called out.

"Faith, do you have to yell?" she asked as she walked over and peeked into my bathroom.

"Look at me, Mom."

I held out my hands, touched my face, and pulled up my shirt to reveal my stomach. Years of cheerleading practices had made my stomach tight. But tight and shockingly white...no thanks.

"My skin is so bland. Please, can I go tan at the gym? I look pale and pathetic."

"Faith Noel Thomas, that is absolutely not true," she said sternly. I saw her glance around my bathroom and room. She was inspecting it.

"It's clean," I said.

"Listen, Babe. I want your self-esteem to go up, not down. You bugged me the same way for makeup. Now you're able to wear a little, and you're still not happy with your appearance. You have to get your worth from within. Know that you're special 'cause you've got the Holy Spirit in you."

I tried to take in what she said. Even though I didn't feel like I was an ugly duckling, I certainly didn't believe I was a swan.

* * * * *

"You're not mad at me, are you?" Nellie's voice startled me.

"Girl, you scared me!" I turned around to see her standing in the hall. "How'd you get here?"

"Rocky let me in."

"Who?"

"Your crazy brother. He told me his new name is Rocky."

I shook my head and threw up my hands. "For a good kid, Blake is so bizarre sometimes. But actually he's been going by Rock, not Rocky."

"Why?"

"He says he is determined to stand on the rock of God."

"That's pretty impressive for a fifth grader," Nellie said.

I pointed toward her. "Let's not get sidetracked here. You hung up on me."

"I know. I'm sorry," she said as she came over to hug me. "I think I'm jealous. I want you all to myself. Niles doesn't deserve you at all. Forgive me?"

I looked at her for a minute and then smiled broadly. Nellie was not easy to stay mad at.

And I was starting to understand her strange behavior. Sort of.

"So you forgive me?" She pointed to my head. "Hey, your hair is even cuter than before. You're cuter than ever. Meanwhile, I'm still ugly me," she said, surprising me with her radical change of topic.

"Nellie, you know I'm glad we're great friends."

"Best friends."

"Okay, best friends, but listen, you need to—"

"Let you do what you want, I suppose? No matter what the consequences are to me?"

She was bringing up Niles again! I rolled my eyes toward the ceiling and started to count for a moment like my mom always did to clear her head before responding to me. Nellie was just as annoyed by this method as I usually was. I could hear her sighing loudly. When I finished counting, I said, "I was going to say that you need to believe that you are very pretty."

"Oh," she said shyly. Then she smiled and said, "Same with you."

"Why do we struggle with that so much? We're smart. We've got style—"

"Yeah!"

"And we believe that God made us just the way He wants us. We have the power of faith and the Holy Spirit, Nellie. You told me all about this last year. So why do we still question our value and our beauty so much?"

She thought about this for a minute and then answered, "I guess because we are human, and for whatever reason we still want other people to think we're beautiful. The world tells us we have to meet a certain standard. I know that isn't what God is asking, but it sure is hard to ignore the image we all have of what pretty and perfect look like."

I nodded. She was right. It was hard to ignore

> **Value Verse**
>
> "Neither death nor life, neither angels nor demons, neither the present nor the future, nor any powers, neither height nor depth, nor anything else in all creation, will be able to separate us from the love of God that is in Christ Jesus our Lord."
>
> [Romans 8:38-39]

the expectations we and others set for ourselves when it came to outward beauty. I realized that this blowup with Nellie had all been about the same thing. We were insecure.

"Nellie?" I said seriously.

"What?"

"I would choose you over your brother if it came down to that, but it shouldn't have to. We're friends, and we can talk through things. Next time, don't be hanging up on me right when we could work out our problems."

"Got it," she agreed.

We'd been through a lot over the past year. Our friendship was as solid as the hug I reached out to give Nellie. All was forgiven.

At the end of last year, my younger sister, Joy, and I were connecting more than usual. She was pretty and confident—probably because she's a top cheerleader and I'm still trying to find my way in the sport. I was getting along better with Blake, aka Rock, too. And after a rough year, my parents seemed closer than ever.

Thinking about all these good things, I thanked God for making us a stronger family. I was with my dad on part of his new tour. He and his popular Christian band had a big concert in Birmingham, Alabama, at the convention center. I hung out backstage as he got ready for the show. Usually he looked so excited to be sharing about God through his music, but today he seemed deep in thought, and it actually scared me a bit. Finally, I asked, "Dad, what's wrong?"

"Oh, Angel! You startled me."

"Dad, you're about to go on, and you seem so…I don't know…not yourself."

"Does my daughter know me or what?" He grabbed both of my hands, trying to reassure me that he was okay, but he couldn't say it because it was clear that he was not.

"Talk to me, Dad. What's wrong? It's not something with you and Mom, is it?"

"We're fine. You're growing up so much, and you want to take care of your dad even though that's not your job. I'm supposed to take care of you."

We sat down on a bench offstage, and he confessed to me his disappointment.

"I was waiting for my parents to show up."

"They're going to come down from Huntsville?"

"They're supposed to."

This actually surprised me because my dad and his parents hadn't been close for a long time. They had some kind of falling out a few years ago. It was so bad that we hadn't been able to see Ma-Ma and Pa-Pa much at all.

"You really wanted them here, didn't you?" I linked my arm through his.

"It would've been nice."

"Keep praying, Dad. God can work it out."

> **Um…um…you must be the new drummer?**

"You're a wise girl." He hugged me just as the announcer called him out on stage. I clapped quietly from where I stood and watched my dad's shoulders relax and his posture of joy return. Without paying attention, I turned around and bumped in to a handsome, twentysomething blond. He was very cute, and he was holding drumsticks. I could feel my face turn red when he flashed a smile at me.

I stammered, "Um…um… you must be the new drummer?"

"Yeah. I'm Drew Parker. Are you Jack Tyler Thomas's younger sister?"

Oh my gosh! Was he saying I didn't look like a little girl? Wow! I thought, *I like this guy.*

"No," I said shyly. "I'm his oldest daughter."

"Darn. You're real cute."

As he walked away, I melted.

School after the Christmas break was, sadly, as difficult as it was before break. My classes were hard, particularly Earth science and algebra. And even though I wouldn't admit it to anyone, I was tired from cheerleading too. It took a lot out of me physically. My coach kept getting onto the team about taking practice seriously. Honestly, workouts were so intense, and today was no exception.

During the first break I sat down with my friend Hope. I didn't see her much around school. We had different classes. I kept bumping into her sister, Holly, all the time. I loved that I could talk to Hope about what was going on with me. We were different colors, but we were connected on many different levels.

"Why isn't your sister like you?" I asked between practice drills.

Hope paused a second to drink some Gatorade. "Don't worry about Holly. She's not really a bully. She's a bluffer. She messes with the people she knows she can annoy. Ignore her in the hallways. I got issues with her too."

"What's going on?" I asked. I could tell by her expression that I had hit a nerve.

JANUARY

SOMETHING TO DO

Pray for good things to happen in the life of someone you don't particularly care for. Pray for peace and prosperity in their life.

THINK ABOUT IT

Think about what you want to get accomplished, and make a New Year's Resolution.

HISTORY LESSON

The first New Year's was not originally on January 1. The holiday was celebrated in Babylon in about 2000 BC. It began with the first visible crescent moon, and lasted 11 days. Each day had a different celebration.

HOLIDAYS

New Year's Day → January 1
Martin Luther King Jr. → January 15

HAPPY BIRTHDAY TO YOU

Orlando Bloom → January 13
Mischa Barton → January 24
Alicia Keys → January 25
Nick Carter → January 28
Wilmer Valderrama → January 30

Faith's Timeline

Jan. 2nd → Argued with Nellie.
3rd → Started Christmas scrapbook. I'm so behind.
5th → Go on Dad's tour with family.
6th → School is back in session. More time off, please!
Mondays, Wednesdays, Saturdays cheer practice—Why do my friends have so many issues? Can we all just quit moaning and cheer already!

> I know the beauty that I have, and the beauty that's inside me.
> — ALICIA KEYS

[blog]

>>

When my day seems to not be working out like I planned, I drop to my knees and pray. Somehow before I get up I feel better knowing God is included in the mix to fix it.

<<

Callie | Beaufort, SC | 13 years old | 8th Grade

"It's my stepmom. You're so lucky you live with both of your parents. I know your folks had issues last year, but they made it through."

I'd forgotten how much I'd told my friend. My dad had messed up by spending time with a woman who was a backup singer in his band last year. His toying with temptation had turned the family upside down for a year. Hope helped me through that, and now I wanted to be here for Hope to help her get through her stuff. "I'm here."

"I hate to admit this, but I borderline hate her. She's nice to me in front of my dad, but as soon as he leaves she's mean. It's crazy. And Dad just doesn't care."

"Back to it, team!" Coach called us to return from break. I said a quick, silent prayer for Hope. I wanted to talk to her while we headed over to the mats, but my friend and teammate Kendal came up to me and immediately let me know that she and I had something to deal with too.

"I hear you're not doing so well in algebra. I'm not getting it either. We should study together—and soon. I'm doing so badly, I might even have to do something crazy to make sure I pass. There's no way I'm repeating that class next year."

I laughed. "What are you talking about?"

Kendal leaned in closer to me and said, "Cheat."

"You wouldn't!"

She shrugged and raised her eyebrows.

"We'll get together and study. God will help us both through it," I told her.

"God? That's your thing apparently, but it isn't mine."

I didn't know how to take her. A part of me wanted to only be with people who believed in the Lord, but the spiritual side of me knew that God wanted me to draw all people unto Him.

"Why do you believe in God?" Kendal asked as we joined the rest of the team.

I didn't hesitate. I stood firm and looked her straight in the eye and said, "Like my name, I have faith. I have faith that He's real."

"So, it's like a hunch to you? No real proof?"

"I walk by faith. God is real to me, and He reveals Himself in my life every day. Things aren't perfect, but they are definitely better."

"Ugh! Good for you then." She jogged to her place on the floor.

I knew her sarcasm well. I'd been the same way before I really needed God and He came through for me. Everything changed at that point. I decided to spend time praying for Kendal. I knew that if my heart could change, her heart could too.

Before we were far into our routine, we heard squeals coming from the other side of the gym.

Please don't let it be broken, Lord, I prayed. We were coming into competition season, and Joy was the star. Everyone needed her to be better. The ambulance and my mom arrived at the same time. My mom followed behind, and they allowed me to ride with Joy. I wiped her tears as she cried.

"Why did this have to happen to me?"

"Calm down," the ambulance man said. "It doesn't look like your foot is broken, but we need to stabilize it until we know for sure."

"Faith, pray for me," Joy said, looking up at me helpless and scared.

I smiled to reassure her and started to pray, "Heavenly Father, I ask You to give my sister comfort. Please make this injury not be a severe one. Take away the pain—"

"And my nose, my nose! Pray for my nose. I don't want it to be broken, or I'll be looking like an ugly duckling," she interrupted me with a whine.

"Call an ambulance!" one of the assistant coaches called out.

"Faith! It's your sister!" Mary, one of my sister's teammates, said as she ran up to me, breathless and pale from anxiety.

I took off running to the other part of the gym and asked the crowd around Joy to step aside. In the center of a small group Joy was wailing on the mat. Blood was gushing from her face. She had one hand to her nose and the other hand was clutching her ankle.

"Hope, get my phone!" I yelled over my shoulder.

I didn't want to send my mom into a panic, but she would want to know immediately that something had happened.

After I hung up with Mom, I kept brushing Joy's hair back and reassuring her. I thought about Kendal and her doubts about God. Her anger about whether God is real or not. Here I was a believer telling someone about Him, and then my sister gets hurt badly. It didn't make me disbelieve, but it certainly made me wonder why God allowed His children to go through pain.

> I needed **God** to show up and give me **help**. Why was I still so uncertain about things when I had God and **His Word** to stand on?

"Let us relax knowing that You understand all our concerns and that You guide us. Lord, please help Joy heal quickly. In Jesus' name we pray and believe. It's done. Amen."

What a dramatic start to the year. Between Nellie's attitude, Hope's pain, Joy's accident, my lack of confidence about my looks, and even Dad's sadness at the concert… it became very clear that having faith did not mean life would be smooth sailing. I needed God to show up and give me help. Why was I still so uncertain about things when I had God and His Word to stand on? I started to pray again. I wouldn't ask for perfection, but I sure needed Him to tweak a few things. It's not that I wasn't happy with the job He was doing, but, honestly, I had pictured things better.

Conquer Point

Okay, so things aren't working out perfectly. Life will have twists and turns. So relax the next time life takes a turn down a path you didn't plan to tread. Use that instance to draw closer to God. The Lord longs to guide your steps.

Prayer

Lord, my life is spinning out of control. One moment I'm fine and the next moment I'm having to deal with some issue. Please give me peace within to not stress so much. Help me know that if I focus on You, my life won't get unmanageable. After all, I'll have You on my side. In Jesus' name, amen.

u Journal

CHAPTER 2:

february

Jumbled Up Inside

Some days I just don't want to move. I want to stay curled up in a ball and let the day pass me by. Don't ask me what I think this accomplishes, but when it all gets mixed up, I need alone time to sort things out. Am I wrong for that?

Does moping around help you?

[CHAPTER 2]

Jumbled Up Inside

The comfort of the big, comfy couch didn't seem to seep into my mood. I was stressed and frustrated. I felt as though a dark cloud was hovering over me. Public school was supposed to be easier than the private school education I'd been used to. That's what everyone told me. I had told myself this same thing. But it wasn't true—not by a long shot. I was struggling more than ever.

I couldn't keep up in algebra and Earth science. Every day the teachers were losing me more and more, and big practice exams were coming up in both subjects. I spread out my papers and books all over my room, hoping that the knowledge might jump out at me and make sense. I was worried that I would never catch up.

Giving up wasn't my nature for school, cheerleading, friendships, or faith. So when that uncontrollable urge to say "It's over…I can't get a grip on it" snuck into my thoughts, it scared me. **Lord, I'm coming to You now asking for help. It's not as if I don't try. It isn't like I waste time partying or cutting class. I'm actually trying, but I still don't get it. Can You help me, please?**

A low rumble of voices started like a drumroll when the science teacher stood in front of the class for a moment with our test papers in hand and then methodically walked the rows and handed the papers back to the students, one by one.

When he got to me, I reached up for the test, but I closed my eyes for a few seconds first. My heart skipped a beat when I saw the big red *F* at the top. I felt a wave of nausea come and go. While other students talked to one another about what they were doing at lunch, I barely held it together. Finally, the bell rang and everyone shuffled out the doors. The hallways I had become used to now seemed strange and full of turns and people I couldn't recognize. I passed by the door to algebra class twice before noticing it. There was no time to decide to close my eyes this time. The teacher, Ms. Johnson, stood by the door and handed us our latest test results as we entered the room.

An *F* was at the top of my folded page.

Good thing my seat was close by because I basically crumpled into it. What was going on? It was like I had stepped from an okay life

into some kind of nightmare. I covered my paper up when the guy sitting behind me tried to look over my shoulder to see what I got. I stared straight ahead, keeping the tears back. As Ms. Johnson got ready to discuss the next section we would be studying, Kendal slid from her seat and walked toward me. I wanted to jet out the door. It wasn't nice… but I sort of hoped Kendal didn't do too well on the test either.

"You're not smiling," she said.

I didn't respond. My thoughts were paralyzed and so was my mouth. I couldn't believe this: two big, fat *F*'s in one day. What were my parents going to say? All of a sudden I felt dizzy, so I dashed out of the room, fled down the hall, drank from the water fountain, and slid down to the floor. Thank goodness nobody saw my ridiculous one-person race for water. I stared at the floor. After a few minutes a pair of high heels entered my frame of vision. I tilted my head up and saw Ms. Johnson looking at me with concern on her face.

"Faith. It's okay."

"No, it's not okay. You don't understand."

"You're going to be able to pull up this grade. You just need to go back a few lessons so that you can build those skills, but we can work at it. Don't fall apart on me."

"It wasn't my only *F* today."

"Well, honey, are you studying at home?"

"Yes! I pay attention in your class, don't I? I could feel myself getting defensive, but I had to let it out. "Have I ever missed a day? I don't talk to anyone in class. I'm in my seat before the tardy bell rings. I pay attention. I take notes. I study! I study!"

"Faith, you've been a model student, but somewhere there's a disconnection, which means we need to work harder at it after

> "My **heart** skipped a **beat** when I saw the **big** red **F** at the top."

school. Seeing how distraught you are tells me how important this is for you to get it right. I want to help you. Can you stay focused enough to conquer algebra? For some kids, it's a tough subject. For others, it's a breeze. Now we know we have to work a little harder. We can do it."

I appreciated her concern, but there was no explanation she or I could give as to why I didn't understand the material. I had to believe that with Christ all things are possible. I felt better resting in my faith. I smiled at my teacher, and she told me to take a few seconds before coming back to class. When she had returned to the room, I stood up and took another drink from the water fountain.

"Hey there," someone said from behind me.

Startled by the voice, I turned around but kept the water running. My finger hit the stream, and it splashed all over my shirt. Niles saw it all, but he didn't laugh at me. He stood there looking at me with calm eyes. A water drop made its way down my chin. I reached up to get it just as Niles did the same. I looked around self-consciously.

"No need to turn away, Faith. You're beautiful."

Value Verse

"So God created man in his own image, in the image of God he created him; male and female he created them."

[Genesis 1:27]

All of these feelings I'd never felt before began to arise within me. It was like butterflies were flying in my stomach. I was already frazzled enough from my tests, but now my stomach churned in a new way. Niles was so great…and yet Nellie didn't want me hanging around him. I was torn.

"I gotta go," I said and started to walk past him.

"Okay," he said a bit startled.

I wanted so badly to turn around to see if he was watching me, but I kept my eyes on the door to algebra class. I was so mixed up. I sure hoped God would point me in the right direction.

> "A water **drop** made its way down my chin. I **reached up** to get it just as **Niles** did the same."

Valentine's Day had arrived. It didn't mean much to me personally, but Blake, Joy, and I were excited because my dad had been planning something special for my mom for weeks. We were all pacing the hallway waiting for her to get home from a meeting with an advertising agency to promote her talent agency and the models she was representing. Since she had just started the business, her hours were sporadic. Joy was hobbling on her tender foot and growing more impatient with every minute that passed beyond six o'clock.

When Mom finally walked in the house, we grabbed her leather bag out of her hands and escorted her to my dad, who was standing in the living room with his arms outstretched, holding a big box of chocolates. Mom walked toward him, reached for the chocolates, and stepped into my dad's embrace. They kissed lightly and looked back at the three of us.

"Mom, we think you should go get comfortable," Joy said the line we planned for her to say. We wanted to get my mom to the master bedroom.

"Good idea." Mom nodded, gave Dad another kiss, clutched her box of sweets, and walked to the master bedroom.

Joy started giggling with anticipation. When Mom got to the doorway she stood speechless for only a few seconds and then yelled, "Oh, my! Jack!" We knew she had seen the floor covered with red, pink, and white rose petals. Dad winked at us and walked up behind Mom. He grabbed her free hand and led her to the dining room through the kitchen. The table, lit with a garden of candles, was set for two. Three men with violins were playing sweet, soft music on the covered balcony just outside the dining room. From our viewpoint in the hall, we could see Mom's face. She was getting teary as they sat down for the catered, gourmet dinner.

"Okay, you two. Basement time for us." I pointed to the downstairs.

We had our own spread waiting for us in the family room. Dad had stocked up on snacks and DVDs so that we'd have a good evening too. Within 20 minutes we had polished off a family-sized bag of chips and were starting on the sub sandwiches from our favorite deli. It was kinda nice just being with my brother and sister. I never thought I would feel that way, but considering how strange Nellie had been lately, I realized that when it came down to it—I was lucky to have my family.

Blake was juggling wadded up napkins when we heard the first sounds of trouble. I thought it was the music because the sound was sort of high pitched, but it didn't take too

SELF—ESTEEM GROWS

I Don't Fit Anywhere

The teenage years can be some of the loneliest years of our lives. Our parents and families don't understand that we can think on our own, and our friends just can't be depended on all the time and for every problem. God didn't create us to be alone. He created us to have a relationship with Him. Sin separated us from Him, which is why we feel empty inside even when we have all that this world has to offer, but we don't have faith. We miss Him, and we need Him to have true and everlasting life. First Peter 1:18–19 says, "For you know that it was not with perishable things such as silver or gold that you were redeemed from the empty way of life handed down to you from your forefathers, but with the precious blood of Christ, a lamb without blemish or defect."

So if you're at a place where something is missing in your life and you are feeling bad about yourself and things around you…try Jesus! Jesus came to pay the price for our sin so we could have a relationship with God the Father. Romans 8:38–39 says that "neither death nor life, neither angels nor demons, neither the present nor the future, nor any powers, neither height nor depth, nor anything else in all creation, will be able to separate us from the love of God that is in Christ Jesus our Lord." When you have Jesus in your life, you are brand new and full of life.

[blog]

>>

When I get lonely, that's when I tell myself I need a tall glass of Jesus Juice. It has some faith, hope, love, and prayer in it. Once I gobble that down, I can relax and feel His holy presence with me.

<<

Charlene | Ithaca, NY | 17 years old | 12th Grade

---

long to realize that it was my mom's voice. Her voice only got high when she was upset. How could the perfect night have turned so quickly?

Blake let a napkin fall to the ground. "Is that what I think it is?"

I nodded.

"Why are they arguing?" Joy looked at me as though I might actually have answers.

I shook my head.

Joy looked concerned. "Faith, go check on them. I can't stand to hear them fight. Go make it better. They actually listen to you these days."

Going back upstairs was the opposite of what I wanted to do. It would've been better to climb out the window and run for Nellie's house. But Blake and Joy were upset, and I was the oldest. I slowly made my way up the stairs and back to the main floor hallway. Mom and Dad had moved from the dining room to their bedroom—probably so they could shut the door to keep us from hearing. A lot of good that did.

"Calm down, honey," my father said to my mom. But she wasn't calming down.

"I just can't believe this," I heard her say. "Why, Jack?"

"Because I think it's causing problems."

I moved to lean in toward the door a bit closer, but I tripped and had to put my hands against the door so that my head wouldn't nail it. I stood up straight and looked down. It was Mom's box of chocolates on the floor. Not a good sign.

Dad opened the door. "Faith, could you give us some space, please? We really need to talk. Everything's fine. Go enjoy your setup downstairs."

"Your father and I have some very different opinions, that's all," Mom said, but it was with a bit of anger and sadness.

I hoped that whatever was going on between the two of them could be fixed. Not believing that was the case, I put on a smile for my brother and sister and walked back downstairs to tell them that things were fine. The arguing subsided, and there seemed to be peace back in the house, but in my heart I doubted whether things had been resolved. Nevertheless, I said, "Blake . . . Joy. They'll work it out. They hit a rough spot, but it was nothing."

Joy pouted and rubbed her ankle, as though our parents' argument had reminded her of her own pain. Blake looked discouraged, but all he said was, "I told you before—my name is Rock."

It was the last weekend in February, and the positive things I had hoped about my parents working it out ended up being true. As curious as I was about what had caused the commotion, I knew it was best not to ask questions. By Friday night, when we all went out to a new barbeque restaurant in town, there weren't any signs of the tensions from Valentine's Day. The trouble between Mom and Dad was gone or well hidden, but after I ate Brunswick stew, there were definite problems between me and my stomach. The entire next day, I was miserable. Just when I thought I would spend the entire weekend in the bathroom, Nellie called me with a proposition.

> **Let's have some girl time. I have so much to tell you.**

"Spend the night with me. Let's have some girl time. I have so much to tell you. Please say you'll come, Faith. You'll feel better over here."

She lived just up the street, but each house had a lot of property, so it was a long stretch between our homes. And we both seemed so busy with school these days, our times together were fewer and fewer. This invitation seemed like a good chance for us to smooth out our friendship's recent rocky path. I had to accept, but my mother wasn't big on last-minute invitations. She'd think I had concocted this whole scheme myself.

"Nellie, my mom's not going to go for that," I told my friend.

"Well, then put her on the phone. I'll ask her."

"She's going to think I put you up to that. No."

"I'll have my mom talk to your mom. She thinks just like her," Nellie said, laughing, and we both handed our phones over to the women who would determine the fate of our evening.

It worked. Within the hour I was knocking on Nellie's door with my overnight bag draped over my shoulder. Mom had driven me because it was after dark and cold.

"Hey, Mrs. Thornton," I said to Nellie's mom as she opened the door and ushered me in. "Mom says hi." I pointed to the driveway where Mom waited in the car to be sure I got in the house okay.

She waved to my mom. They had become pretty good friends over the past year. My mom didn't have a lot of girlfriends, so I was really glad they had met. Mrs. Thornton called out to my mom, "We'll send her home tomorrow. She'll be fine."

I followed behind Nellie quickly to avoid small talk with her mom. I really liked Mrs. Thornton, but I was shy, and I didn't like to answer the questions parents asked about life and especially about school. The thought of my lousy grades made me as sick as last night's dinner. I glanced around to remind myself where all the bathrooms were, just in case.

"What are you looking for?" Nellie asked a bit sharply.

"I haven't been over in a while," I said, not wanting to confess my real reason.

"You're looking for Niles, aren't you? After all our talk about that, I can't believe you're here looking around for my brother. Just say it, Faith. You have the hots for him."

I could tell it was not worth stringing out this conversation, so I tried to cut her off early. "Quit being paranoid. I'm not looking for your brother."

"He's not here tonight anyway. He'll be out late as usual. Can you believe he hangs out at the bowling alley with some of his friends? They think they can pick up girls there. Trust me. He's not the one you want to talk to."

"Nellie! I hear ya. Get over it." I was mad. Nellie still wanted to rule me.

"Okay! I was just testing you," she said with a calmer attitude.

I followed her to her room and was surprised to see that she had repainted it. It was very cool with shades of chocolate brown and mint green. Nellie was so self-conscious about everything in her life that she hadn't even mentioned the new paint job. She did look at me expectantly the minute I walked in, though, as if waiting for my approval. Nellie and I had our differences, but we both struggled with this same need. There were times when I had to hear that I was doing well, that things would be okay, that I was worth something.

"I love your room, Nellie. You have such great taste."

Nellie smiled at that and seemed to relax a little too. We both collapsed on her bed. I was feeling weak from not eating much all day, and Nellie seemed preoccupied. We were lost in our individual thoughts until she propped her head up on her hand and said, "Now we can have girl talk?"

"What other kind could we have?" I teased.

My friend's face became very serious. "I've got to tell you about Ethan."

Ethan was the guy Nellie had been hanging out with quite a bit. Her mom was strict about her not dating this young, but Nellie and Ethan still seemed to find ways to be together. I was happy that she liked a guy, but I wasn't sure about Ethan. I figured he was a passing crush.

I was wrong.

"I want to take things to the next level with him."

"Like officially date?"

Nellie looked down at the bedspread and then back to me. "I mean physically."

My stomach had just started to ease up, but now I felt sick emotionally. She was only in the ninth grade. I knew some girls who had sex this young, but, come on, they always regretted it. She didn't even know this guy. I wanted to knock her in the head.

> "I want to take things to the next level with him."

I was trying to figure out how to help Nellie process all of this when she said, "Why are you looking at me like that? You're so judgmental. I was just being honest with the one person I thought was a friend. If I wanted that look, I could've talked to my mom."

"Well, maybe you should talk to your mom."

"Yeah, right! Faith, you may be able to talk to your mom about stuff, but my mom would have a cow if I brought up sex."

"And why do you think that is?"

"I'm sure you'll tell me."

"For one thing, he's your first crush, not the guy of your future. You don't even know Ethan very well. Sex right now would be all about the wrong things."

"I'm not saying I'm going to do it today, but I'm thinking about it, okay? Ethan thinks I'm pretty. I feel good when I'm around him. I want to let him know how great I think he is."

FEBRUARY

SOMETHING TO DO
Send flowers to a friend or family member wishing them a happy Valentine's Day.

THINK ABOUT IT
Attend a True Love Waits (abstinence) Conference, or pledge to stay pure till marriage.

HISTORY LESSON
Saint Valentine was said to be a priest who served during the third century in Rome. He performed secret marriages after the emperor outlawed marriages, stating that single men made better soldiers than ones with wives and families.

HOLIDAYS
Groundhog Day → February 2
Valentine's Day → February 14

HAPPY BIRTHDAY TO YOU
Ashton Kutcher → February 7
Kelly Rowland → February 11
Jennifer Love Hewitt → February 12

Faith's Timeline
Feb. 5th → Got tests back. What a failure!
14th → Parents back at the arguing thing again.
28th → Sleepover at Nellie's house.
Mondays, Wednesdays, Saturdays: cheer practice

I think we are ready to know that there are going to be people who are ready to save the world, who come out when you're in trouble and make sure that you're okay.

— JENNIFER LOVE HEWITT

"Nellie, you and I have God. We don't need guys to give us our value."

Nellie's expression went from openness to complete bitterness. "Quit being jealous just because you don't have anybody."

I couldn't believe she said that to me. I was trying to help my friend, but she obviously didn't really want to hear the truth. I stood up from the bed and pointed a finger at her. "I think it's a stupid idea, and if you don't want a friend who's real and can tell you what she thinks, then maybe I should just go!" I grabbed my bag and made for her door.

I don't know if I thought she was going to stop me, but she didn't. So I kept walking. Every time I gave Nellie the benefit of the doubt, she made me rethink it. Why did I have to have a friend who was all jumbled up inside?

Conquer Point

Life won't always be perfect, and that's okay. Remember, only the Lord knows the bigger picture. So when your world seems all mixed up, just lay it at God's feet. Your soul can rest even with chaos all around you.

Prayer

Heavenly Father, I'm trying hard here to do the right things, say the right things, and follow Your path for my life. However, it's getting harder to understand why things are even more of a mess. Help me to relax and know that even though things seem crazy, You are still in control. Help me maintain my faith in the midst of my storms.

In Jesus' name, amen.

u Journal

CHAPTER 3:

march

Focused on Him

How can you stay focused when you're nervous? How can you maintain composure when you're angry? How can you hide your true feelings when those emotions are just longing to come out? I don't have a clue. But I'm happy to say I know the One who does. Read on.

Maybe the Lord can help us both out.

[CHAPTER 3]

Focused on Him

Nellie was so difficult. Didn't she want an honest friend who could tell her when she was about to make a mistake? I stormed down the hallway with my overnight bag in hand, and as I turned a corner, I ran smack into Niles. I froze.

My heart fluttered and my eyes scanned him from head to toe. I felt so bashful. I couldn't look up again. I held my head down and turned back toward Nellie's door, contemplating whether or not to go back and apologize, even though I knew I was right. At least it would get me out of the hallway and out of Niles's presence.

I felt his strong hand touch my back. "Sorry if I startled you, Faith."

"Oh!" I replied without turning around to face him. "It's okay. I didn't mean to keep you from what you were doing."

"Can we talk for a second? You look upset. Please?"

I took a deep breath and slowly turned toward him. I knew I looked a mess, and I hated every minute of him having to see me looking like such a bum. I tried fixing my hair after I placed my bag down. And then I was mad at myself for caring so much. What had I just told Nellie about getting our value from God?

He leaned toward me and said, "You get embarrassed easily. I don't know why. I think you always look so…" Niles paused as if unsure whether he should say it. "Amazing."

I didn't feel amazing, but after he said it, I did feel a little more confident.

"I didn't know you were spending the night," he said.

"I *was* spending the night, but now I'm heading home."

"What? Nellie getting on your nerves?"

I didn't want to talk about his sister, but I also didn't want to lie. I stayed quiet.

"Look, let's go in the kitchen. My mom's homemade peanut butter cookies smell good! Don't you want some?"

"I am pretty hungry. I've been sick all day, so I could use some food about now."

"Right this way," he said, smiling.

"I thought you were at the bowling alley." **Checking out girls**, I almost said.

Niles looked at me with a look of confusion. "Did Nellie say that?"

I shrugged. I should just be quiet because I was going to cause problems if I got between brother and sister.

> **"** If I guarded **my heart** now and nipped these feelings in the bud, **then** I'd be **protected**. **"**

"I don't hang at the bowling alley. That's where Ethan, Nellie's love disaster, hangs out. That's hardly my crowd. Those guys are so…" Niles stopped himself short and shook his head. I knew he wasn't going to get any further into this conversation. Even though I was curious as to what he was going to say, I knew it was probably best to drop the topic.

Niles pointed to the cookies and I sat down. What in the world was I doing? What was I allowing myself to be a part of? Sitting down with a guy I sort of had feelings for was not a good idea. Nellie would blow a fuse if she saw me, and I was a little afraid of being alone with her brother.

All the things Nellie wanted to do with her guy weren't things I was thinking about for myself, but would being with Niles change that? If I guarded my heart now and nipped these feelings in the bud, then I'd be protected. That was important.

"I shouldn't be here alone with you," I told him. The only light we had on was a night-light above the kitchen counter. I reached for a cookie from the platter on the table.

"I like you, Faith," he said, getting up and moving behind me to turn on the light switch. "I want to get to know you. Just think about it."

When I turned to face him, he was gone.

"I see you didn't get too far," Nellie said as she came into the kitchen a minute later. "They're good, huh?"

I couldn't focus on what she was asking me or even how great the cookie tasted. I still had Niles's words floating in my brain. He liked me! When he said "think about it," what in the world did that mean? Think about hanging

BEHIND THE SCENES
ON NILES

FULL NAME: Niles Austin Thornton
BIRTH DATE: March 25
FAMILY MAKEUP: Dad, Mom, twin sister, Nellie
FAVORITE COLOR: Green
FAVORITE FOOD: Burgers
HOBBIES: Football
GOALS: Excel at sports. Get to know Faith. To do better in school.
STRENGTHS: Nice guy
WEAKNESS: Sometimes he gives up trying for what he wants.
ONE POSITIVE ABOUT THIS CHARACTER: Kindhearted
WORD OF INFLUENCE: Strong
FAVORITE PHRASE: Dream bigger

with him? Or think about my feelings? What was I going to do if Nellie found out?

"So you're ignoring me? I'm glad you're not gone. I'm a jerk. You were just telling me how you feel. And one day you'll understand. I know I'm supposed to live my life to please God, but there's something new going on inside me, Faith. I can't explain it, but I don't want you to think that I don't respect your opinions and advice. Please stay. We'll enjoy the rest of the night without talking about boys. Or school. Or parents. Or siblings. Let's eat, watch movies, paint our nails, and talk girl talk… except the things I listed. I guess that leaves clothes to talk about…or your scrapbooking maybe?" Nellie laughed.

Just then we heard a door shut somewhere in the house. Nellie looked at me funny. "Was Niles down here?"

"Let's take these cookies and go watch some movies," I said quickly.

Following Nellie back to her room, I caught myself smiling when I thought about what Niles had said to me. It was like we were playing tennis, and he served the ball to my court. Was I going to hit it back? That was a question I couldn't answer. I was thankful that Nellie and I were good again. Friendship was tough but worth it.

* * * * *

My dad and his band were working on a new album. He had invited me to sit in during their recording, and I was more than happy to join him. I loved the feel of the studio. Sitting in a chair and watching him play his guitar was a sight to see. "On Him I Stay Focused" was a slow song on the new album. The soothing song helped me to understand what God wanted from me: to keep Him first above all things; to remember that He guides my steps; to know, trust, and believe that He is the author and finisher of my faith; and to comprehend

that as long as I stay focused on Him, "Forever I'll have peace." This was the last line of the song, and as soon as they sang it, I felt the truth of it.

I didn't even realize that I was saying the words, but I guess I was singing along as the group ran through the song for a second time. When the music from the band stopped, everybody was looking over at me. As soon as I realized it, I turned away.

"Come here, Faith," my dad called. "Sing that again."

"No, Dad, that's okay."

"Go ahead, sweetheart. It's just us."

"Well, if she sings half as good as she looks, you might not have a job," Drew Parker said out loud.

> **"Our talents from God are for us to use, to share, to grow, and to give back to God."**

Value Verse

"In all these things we are more than conquerors through him who loved us."

[Romans 8:37]

"And if you keep noticing the way my teenage daughter looks, you won't have a job," my dad said rather sternly. Everybody in the room jumped back.

I remember when I first met the drummer back in January. I had thought he was cute, and I liked that he thought I was older. But today's comment left me with a sick feeling in my stomach. His attention was not what I was after, that was for sure.

"Dad, I can't sing," I whispered in my father's ear when I was in the recording part of the studio. "I'm just here to listen, okay? Please don't put me on the spot."

"Don't worry about everyone here. Sing for God. I heard you last Christmas, Faith. You can do it."

He started the music, and I couldn't get the first note out. I hated that my dad put me in that position. Why'd he have to make me a part of the act? Embarrassed and unable to try again out of fear of failing, I dashed out of the room. It was the panic I had felt when I got the tests back with the big fat *F*'s on them. I couldn't breathe.

I sank down in a chair in their kitchen. I had let Dad down, and I'd let the Lord down...all because I had no confidence in myself. I heard Dad in the doorway, but I didn't want to look up.

"Please go back to practice," I pleaded. "I know you guys are getting ready to cut an album. Don't waste your time on me. I don't need a babysitter."

"It's okay, Faith. I'm sorry I pushed you. It's just that I saw something in you that I wanted to come out, but if you're not ready to share your talent, I understand. I'm the one who should be apologizing. I'm sorry. Forgive me?"

"Dad!" I said as I got up and rushed into his arms. "Thank you. I just don't wanna let you down."

"You didn't let anyone down." He hugged me tightly and then pushed me away from him slightly so that he could look me in the eye. "Faith, I love you so much. You could never let me down, but I do worry that maybe you are letting yourself down if you allow the enemy to defeat your dreams. In the Bible there is the parable of talents. Basically, Jesus told a story about a master who has to leave his home for a while. So he hands some talents to some of his servants. These talents are a measure of money. Two of the men took what was given them and made more. But one guy just hid his money, afraid that something might happen to it. When the master returned and heard from the man who did nothing because he had been afraid, he took the money back and gave it to one of the others."

I thought about this for a few seconds and nodded. "Our abilities are like those gifts of money from the master, right?"

"Yes. Our talents from God are for us to use, to share, to grow, and to give back to God. If we never use them because we're afraid, we will never know what God intended them to become. Don't hide your talent, Faith. Use it to glorify our heavenly Father. You've gotta feel comfortable with that. You've gotta stay so wrapped up in how you feel about God that the notes just come out and the insecurities fade away."

"Dad, how do you get the courage to sing in front of thousands?"

"I think about sharing my love for God with each person in the audience, and then it doesn't seem like a crowd at all. And each time I sing,

> # [blog]
>
> ❯❯
>
> When my best friend and I committed to hold each other accountable to God's Word, my life has never been better.
>
> ❮❮
>
> Laura | Troy, AL | 14 years old | 9th Grade

it's really me singing for God, honoring Him, and giving Him glory."

"You say I have talent, but why can't I believe that?"

"That's why you need to pray about seeing yourself differently."

"God would have to do something pretty radical to get me to see myself any differently. All I know is the fear inside me. All I see are the parts of me I don't like or I want to change. Some days I'm confident, but mostly I struggle to maintain a sense of getting through." I stopped myself before I could confess about my bad grades.

"When I keep my eyes on God, I know He'll work out the rest for me," said Dad. "I'm not as strong as you think I am. When I let the Holy Spirit in me shine, my strength becomes God's strength, and I know that I can do anything. And Faith, so can you. Our confidence is in Christ."

I hugged my dad tightly. He'd given me a lot to think about. Though I spent the rest of the day still watching, inside I knew God was doing something with my heart. I couldn't wait to see what that turned out to be.

✻ ✻ ✻ ✻ ✻

I was really excited that Hope invited me over to her house after a cheer practice so that I could hang out on a Saturday. We were actually going to study. I loved being around Hope because she had the confidence I knew I lacked. She seemed so on fire about life. Nothing seemed to intimidate her. I wanted a bit of that confidence.

"How do you stay so on beat all the time?" I asked her while we munched on popcorn and read through our math notes. Hope was a good student, and I was thankful that she was there to help me with my weaker subjects.

"I'm not telling you that I have it all down or that I've figured out life, because that's a big field. I've got so much drama going on in my life, Faith. I try not to let it show, but deep inside it's eating me up. It's hard for me."

"What's hard for you?"

Hope motioned around her. "This house is hard. Watching my stepmom with her kids and with Dad while my sister and I live here too. I see him do more for those babies than he has ever done for us. My mom is living somewhere in the projects because every time my dad gives her money, she blows it on stuff that she has no business buying. It's just hard for me 'cause I wanna help her, but my mom stole from me."

I didn't want to ask her, but Hope could see in my eyes that there was something else I wanted to say. She said, "Go ahead. Ask me anything."

"Is your mom an addict?"

"She was. I don't know if she still is or not. I do know that part of the reason for the addiction was her devastation when Dad left her. They tried to work some things out last year, but it wasn't good. Mom wasn't too stable even

> "I don't know what people have told you, **girl**, but your rhythm is **whack**."

before Dad messed up. When she gave him an ultimatum, he didn't choose her, and her life fell apart. Now I'm living here with this lady. It's just a total disaster, Faith."

I saw my friend's eyes tear up, and I desperately wanted to do something, anything to help ease her pain. I reached over and placed my hand on her back. Even though I couldn't change things, it felt good to be able to offer her comfort.

Our time together was going by so quickly. We had ordered pizza as our break from homework, and once we had eaten most of it, we decided to dance around her room. I was so off beat, even I had to laugh. With all the cool moves Hope was doing, I wanted to join in. All of a sudden the music stopped.

I turned around to see Holly standing by the CD player, looking at me with disgust. "Your little white friend needs some help. You better take her back to elementary classes 'cause she's not handling the accelerated version at all. I don't know what people have told you, girl, but your rhythm is whack."

"We were having fun, Holly. Why do you have to be so mean to Faith? You know she's got the moves and the talent." Hope stood up for me right away. Holly looked surprised.

"She's probably just using you to learn new grooves, Hope. I wouldn't be bettin' on her friendship just yet. I'm glad she stood up for you on the cheerleading team last year… but like I said, I wouldn't count on her to have your back forever. Ya know?"

"Hey!" Now it was my turn to stand strong. But one look from Holly and I backed up a few steps. The girl was gorgeous but mighty tough.

"Holly, get out of here!" Hope said as she threw a pillow toward the door.

My mood was deflated. I plopped down on the floor, unwilling to try again.

Hope looked at me and pursed her lips together with a look of attitude. "What? You gonna give up now? Girl, my sister is just jealous that you're all that, and that you pick up way better than her."

"Don't try to cheer me up. I'm not even close to your level, and your sister knows it. I know it. I can't dance."

"Can't? That is not a word we're going to use. And truth be told, Faith, my sister had it tough in middle school. She was on a cheer squad where she was the only black girl, and she got ragged on a lot. She felt like they just used her to show off, and they didn't really care about her as a person. She's all attitude ever since."

"But not everyone would've treated her that way. I wouldn't have."

"I know. I'm just praying for her… that she'll be herself and stop acting up so much. She's going to get herself in trouble."

"We're supposed to be Christians. How come life is so hard, Hope?"

Focused on Him | 37

"Maybe it's 'cause we're not in God's Word enough, so we don't stay connected to Him."

She sat down next to me. She had her issues, and I had mine. We decided to hold hands and pray about our lives, our families, and our need to connect with God more. She told me that in her church they talked about accountability partners.

"What's that?" I asked.

"It's where you get with somebody that's on your same level in Christ, and y'all hold each other up to make sure each does what God would want. You follow God's rule by encouraging that person and stuff like that. You wanna be mine?"

The prospect of having somebody push me along in my faith was so exciting. "That's exactly what I need. Someone as strong as me to push me along when I need it. Yeah, let's do it!"

We both jumped up and down. She turned on one of her dad's new cool gospel tunes. I began to dance again with my friend Hope. We were going to be accountability partners, helping each other stay focused on Him.

Conquer Point

It may be hard to follow God when there are so many pressures pulling at you to do the wrong thing. Find friends who love the Lord and hang with them. Ask God for help when you feel weak. God won't leave you or forsake you.

Prayer

God, I am weak, and I need You to help me stay strong. Help me through tough situations and let me make You proud with my choices. I want to study Your Word and praise Your name, but I need You to help me give up my desires and get on board with Your will.

In Jesus' name, amen.

MARCH

HOLIDAYS
St. Patrick's Day → March 17

HAPPY BIRTHDAY TO YOU
Bow Wow → March 9
Carrie Underwood → March 18
Sarah Jessica Parker → March 25
Julia Stiles → March 28

SOMETHING TO DO
Find something with a four-leaf clover on it (bookmark, coin, card, etc.). Maybe if you're lucky, you'll find a real one.

THINK ABOUT IT
Remember to wear green on St. Patrick's Day so you don't get pinched.

HISTORY LESSON
St. Patrick was a missionary who was regarded as a patron saint.

Faith's Timeline

March 1st → Niles saw me at 12:01 A.M.
10th → My dad wants me to sing with him. I can't.
23rd → Hope and I agree to become accountability partners. Wow! Keeping each other strong in the Word is our vow to one another. Hope we stay true to it.
25th → Niles' birthday
Mondays, Wednesdays, Saturdays: cheer practice

> I don't judge others. I say if you feel good with what you're doing, let your freak flag fly.
> — SARAH JESSICA PARKER

CHAPTER 4:

april

Lacked the Confidence

Do you struggle with life as much as I do? Sometimes I think I'm the only one who feels totally inadequate. Why is it so difficult to feel sure? Is there some secret to finally feeling secure and loved?

I plan to find out.

[CHAPTER 4]
Lacked the Confidence

As I stood in front of the full-length mirror in my room, I wondered what outfit to wear today. I wasn't happy about my body these days. I wished I looked more like Nellie or Hope. They looked like high school girls. In spite of what Dad's drummer said, I knew I looked more like I was 11 than a teenager, let alone able to pass for my dad's younger sister.

I stared at my clothing selections. They were Christmas gifts that I had loved when I opened them, but now, as I stood facing the mirror with them, I wasn't sure. The red-and-brown ensemble didn't look the best on me. Neither did the yellow outfit. The latest style was to wear fitted shrugs over a longer shirt. I felt so abnormal sometimes that I at least wanted my clothes to be on trend. It was a tricky thing, though, because kids at school showed no mercy. You wear the wrong thing, and you get ostracized. You wear something that's too flashy, and then you get drummed for thinking you're the bomb. It's a no-win.

Parents don't understand that being a teenager is hard. Sure, we don't have to pay the bills, work a 9–5 job, or deal with marriage issues, but trust me, if any parent had to walk in a teen's shoes today, they would see that it is much harder than when they were growing up.

"Lord, why am I so unhappy with my appearance? Is it normal, or am I crazy? I'm asking You to help me get over this insecurity. I know that it keeps me from stepping up and being stronger in You. Amen."

"Who are you talking to, sweetie?" I heard my mom say as she came to my door. "Oh! You're trying on the outfits. They both look so cute!" I couldn't believe she was pointing to the one I had just ruled out. "Okay, what's with your frowning face? You don't like it? Joy liked everything I got her, and I was sure that I had chosen great matches for your style too."

Of course Joy would like everything Mom picked out for her. She was almost my size, and she was in the seventh grade. I was the ninth grader with barely any chest and definitely no curves to fill out any of my jeans. No wonder Niles liked me. He probably thought of me as one of the boys...one of his pals.

"They're fine, Mom."

"No, Faith. I'm not just talking about the clothing. What is going on with you? You seem unhappy and stressed. Anything we could talk about?"

My mom had been busy over the last several months getting her talent agency up and running. She'd signed a good number of models, including some of the girls from my school, but I knew all that was still stressful. I didn't want to add to her stuff right now.

"Mom, I said I'm cool."

> **Value Verse**
> "I can do everything through him who gives me strength."
> [Philippians 4:13]

She took my hand and led me over to my bed and sat me down. I knew she was headed for a mother-daughter talk. I wasn't ready to tell her everything that was going on. I'd missed our deep talks and probably could use one about now. Still, I wasn't sure whether I wanted to spill my guts about how pathetic my life was and how sick I was of doubting how I looked, how I acted, and who I was.

To my amazement my mom honed in on what was wrong. She stroked my hair. "Baby, you know you're beautiful, right?"

"No, Mom, I'm not," I said, hating that she kept telling me stuff that I knew wasn't true. "I have these braces. Brunette hair is in, and I'm a blonde. My body looks like I should still be in middle school. You might think I'm cute… like a little girl is cute or a puppy wearing a hat is cute. But I am not beautiful."

"Oh, Faith. How do you not see what I see? You are a physical beauty, and you are amazingly strong, resilient, and lovely from the heart. Do you get how rare that is?"

"As rare as a puppy wearing a hat?" I said with a half smile.

Mom slapped her hand on her thigh and then snapped her fingers. "You don't believe me? Well, then how about we put a wager on it?"

"What do you mean?" I asked. She was always up to something. The good thing and the bad thing about Mom was that she used her creativity to get us to learn something. Her motivational tactics worked when I was younger, but this was different. She couldn't change my body or my mind with some game.

"My talent agency is starting to do well. People are calling, and we need some more models."

Joy had started to do some modeling for my mom. I had no interest in that scene. Who wants a bunch of people telling you what is wrong with you? I could do that to myself. "No, thanks. If you are even offering me a chance to model. Or are you offering me a chance to do filing and run errands for the pretty girls?"

"Faith, sarcasm does not become you. But that's okay, because what I am about to tell you might just change your mind about all of this."

Mom paused to build up the excitement, but the excitement was only on her end. I was filling with dread.

She continued. "I just got a new casting call for something I think you would be really good at. This would give me a chance to prove to you that you really are more than gorgeous."

I was intrigued at that point. I sat up a little straighter and ran my fingers through my hair, not apologetically or shyly, but with more confidence than I was feeling just a few minutes ago. Could my mom really have an idea to help me?

"I want to enter a few girls in the Miss Teen Nashville pageant."

What? I slouched down and returned to my pity party. "No, Mom," I said before she took it any further.

"Faith, wait. You think I'm just saying that because of how you are feeling right now. But

I've been looking for some girls who are pretty, confident, outgoing, and talented. The only girl I'm certain of for this contest is you."

"No, no, and no." I shook my head repeatedly. She obviously did not understand my tragic state of being.

"Faith, say you'll think about it. I know you'd place in the top ten with the training I've received in pageants and your natural abilities. You know I'll go overboard for my own precious daughter. Just give it a shot."

"I promise *only* to think about it."

> " I just got a new **casting call** for something I think you would be **really good** at. "

"You could always do it purely to try and prove me wrong." She smiled at this and I had to laugh. But I still wasn't convinced.

It was such a crazy idea! No way did I have the nerve to do anything like that.

* * * * *

Easter and spring break had come and gone. I enjoyed the break and loved being able to spend some quiet time with God. I studied the Twenty-third Psalm a lot. I wanted to dissect it, understand it, and make it something I lived.

It was hard to get past the first part: **The LORD is my Shepherd, I shall not be in want.** My problem was that I did want. I did feel like I was lacking. I wanted things of the world that were apart from Christ. This was a tough one to embrace. If I focused on Him, those worldly things wouldn't be so important;

I'd be full and have everything I wanted. I was struggling because I truly wasn't full. Not yet.

I will fear no evil, for you are with me; your rod and your staff, they comfort me. As thankful as I was that God was working out so many things in my life, I was still full of fear. I couldn't get those bad grades out of my mind. I dwelled on Nellie's behavior toward me and her brother, and I worried about what choices she might make just because she didn't feel good about herself. When I thought about Jesus dying for my sins so that I could be in heaven forever, I felt loved—but how do you keep that sense of being loved?

When break was over and we all returned to school, I was right back where I was before… the reality of life and my potential failures.

"Faith, do you have the answer?" Ms. Johnson asked, putting me on the spot.

I didn't want kids laughing at me if I answered wrong. I pretended to drop my pencil so I could stall. By the time I sat back up, she had called on someone with confidence and brains. After class was over, I tried to be the first one out the door, but Ms. Johnson called me over to her desk.

"Faith, you will have to get more studying done at home. I need you to feel good about your answers when I call on you. I suspect you know the answers but are lacking confidence because of your past test scores. I'm willing to work with you, but change will require you to help yourself, take a few risks, and give yourself a real chance to master the unknown." She looked at me with fondness, and I felt a sense of relief. She wasn't scolding me. She was trying to help.

"Yes, ma'am," I told her.

When I walked out of the classroom, Kendal came up to me and said, "You wanna study this stuff together? I don't get it either."

My first thought was that studying with someone who didn't understand math either

APRIL

HOLIDAYS
April Fool's Day → April 1

HAPPY BIRTHDAY TO YOU
Amanda Bynes → April 3
Mandy Moore → April 10
Hayden Christensen → April 19
Kelly Clarkson → April 24

SOMETHING TO DO
Play a joke on a friend or family member.

THINK ABOUT IT
With all the rain, figure out a way to keep yourself occupied.

HISTORY LESSON
April 13, 1743: Thomas Jefferson, the third President of the U.S., was born in Virginia.

Faith's Timeline
April 4th → Mom asked me to enter some pageant. Yuck!
10-14th → Study for exams. So hard!
20-25th → Competition cheerleading tryout week at school. Hope I make it.
26th → I made the squad!
Mondays, Wednesdays, Saturdays: cheer practice

God will never give you anything you can't handle, so don't stress.
— KELLY CLARKSON

[blog]

›› I love memorizing scriptures because I face adversity, I can recall what it says in the Bible and I can overcome. ‹‹

Rae | London, England | 15 years old | 10th Grade

wasn't going to help me. But I didn't say that to her. I just sighed.

"What? You don't wanna study with me?"

"It's not that," I said, realizing I should be sensitive to my friend's feelings. "I just don't think we could help each other. It'd totally be the blind leading the blind."

"Yeah, but we could read the material together and go through it. We can help each other learn it, and then be the only ones in the class who do know it. It'll be fun. Come on, Faith. Let's try."

I don't know why I agreed, but the next afternoon we were at my house. I was trying to study, but she was a little distracted. I don't know why I even bothered inviting her over.

"Kendal, we're supposed to be studying."

"I know, but your house is so beautiful. You don't understand. I don't live like this. Every room is perfect. I love all the colors and the designs. Your house even smells good. Your mom's so nice, making us snacks and all. I could stay here forever."

"There'll be an empty space for you to take if I don't start bringing my grades up. My parents will send me to boarding school." I felt the panic rising up in me. The worries I had tried to stuff the past few weeks were coming out in full force to Kendal. "They think that public school is corrupting my mind, but the truth is that school is fine. I'm just sidetracked and totally offbeat in every area of my life. The material is not sticking with me. This really is not the time for sightseeing."

"Okay, okay. I'm sorry." She finally sat down after being at my home for about an hour. "I just can't believe you have a fireplace on your deck. It's amazing!"

I thought we were going to study. Not! Eventually I gave up, and the two of us just started talking. When her mom came to pick her up, I was actually glad. I wanted to do better in school. I wanted to be the person the teacher called on and who had the correct answer. I wanted to press on and use my abilities like the faithful servants in the parable Dad talked about.

The next day in class, the teacher called on me again. Unfortunately, she got the same response. I didn't want to answer the question. After class I got stopped for another conference.

"So, you're not going over this material, are you?"

I shrugged. "I tried studying with another classmate yesterday, and it didn't help. I don't know where the disconnection is."

"How about you come to school early one day next week and we work together?"

"You'd do that?" I asked, surprised. I figured her help would be extra homework or something like that. She nodded and then I did something I never thought I would do—I embraced a teacher! Though I didn't know any more math, I felt better.

The Twenty-third Psalm was coming alive in

my life and that was exciting! I just wondered how long it would stay.

* * * * *

Two weeks later, when my teacher called on me in class, I could raise my hand and have the correct answer. I was feeling like a new person. I was walking down the hall with Kendal when Hope called us over to look at something on the wall.

"Hey," I said to her.

"Hey, y'all," she responded back.

"What do you got there?" Kendal asked her.

"It's cheerleading tryouts at the school."

"I don't wanna be a school cheerleader!" Kendal said. "I want to compete. I don't want to support losing sports teams. Nope. Not interested."

"Wait, Kendal, don't be so darn quick to judge everything," Hope said. "They're forming a competition squad next year."

All three of us read the flyer with more interest. "But how can I make the squad? Certainly they want a lot less of the stiff routines I was using at the gym. I don't know, Hope. You know I don't have those types of skills," I found myself whining.

"It's a squad, girl. You know they're going to need her skills, yours, and mine," she said, pointing to us one by one.

> **The worries I had tried to stuff the past few weeks were coming out in full force to Kendal.**

"I don't know…"

"Just think about it. I swear, you two are overreactors. Why not try it?" Hope was egging us on, I could tell.

I **was** a little tired of the same routines at the gym. Not that being a member of United Storm wasn't an awesome thing, but I'd been there and done that. Now I wanted to step out and explore my options and my abilities. Maybe… maybe I could do this.

Hope could tell I was still unsure. "It'd be a lot of fun for us all to be on this squad, and we'd be able to set the tone for things because we'd be the first competitive squad here ever."

"Who's to say we'll all make it?" Kendal said with a hint of negativity.

"Well, who's to say we won't?" I chimed in, shocking myself.

"That's the spirit I'm talking about," Hope said, lifting up her hand to give me five. "My girl, Faith! We can do it, guys."

Later that day I knocked on my mom's office door in our basement. She'd made her space so cozy and cute. There was even a separate

> "The day of **tryouts** finally came, but to my **surprise** I was so **second-guessing** myself."

side entrance for when people came to visit her, but it looked like it was supposed to be in a high-rise.

"Am I disturbing you, Mom? You got a sec?"

"For my lovely daughter, but of course!" she said, motioning for me to sit in front of her. "You're gonna do the pageant!"

"Mom!" I said, not wanting to be pressured by it at all.

"Sorry. You go ahead with what you wanted to say."

"The school is starting a competition cheerleading squad."

"Wow! That's impressive."

"And I really think I want to be on the team. Well, I want to try out, and I want to make it. But I also know it will still be a real challenge. Hope and Kendal are planning on trying out too."

"Well, what's the problem?"

"Would it be a crime if I didn't do United Storm next year?"

"Who's to say you can't do both?"

She didn't know about my grades. And by the time she did, I'd be fortunate to have either one of them as extracurricular activities. "School is getting tougher," I said, which was true. "I don't want to overextend myself."

Mom was beaming at me. "I'm so proud that you know what you can and cannot handle. It's good that you're trying something different. When are tryouts?"

"All next week. We learn a new routine and dance, and then we do the actual tryout next Friday."

"I'm behind you with whatever you decide to do."

The day of tryouts finally came, but to my surprise I was so second-guessing myself. Usually if I practiced something thoroughly, I felt in control enough to have a bit of confidence. I hadn't missed a practice all week. And Hope and Kendal were beside me every step of the way.

Eventually it was our turn. They called the three of us out to perform and the music started, but I just stood still. I wanted to break down and cry, run away and hide. I wanted to hit myself over the head with a hammer. The way I froze was ridiculous! I couldn't explain it or shake it off. It was a total flashback of one of my competitions from last year. I thought I was past this kind of fear when performing. What was wrong with me?

I watched the rest of them perform for ten counts. All of a sudden I heard the coach yell,

SELF-ESTEEM GROWS

Who Am I?

You were created with an identity in Christ Jesus. You were made to be like Him. "God created man in his own image, in the image of God he created him; male and female he created them" (Genesis 1:27). So, you are royalty with the authority that goes with it (Genesis 1:26). None of us is perfect. All of us were born with a sinful nature. But the good news is that since we were made to be like God, we can, with His help, be transformed to be more like Him. Whatever sin or "identity crisis" you are battling, you don't have to embrace it. You can overcome it by letting Christ work through you. You are an overcomer! God says that "in all these things we are more than conquerors through him who loved us" (Romans 8:37). In other words, you can do everything through Him who gives you strength (Philippians 4:13).

"Cut! Cut the music. Number 13, do you want to do this?"

There was nothing nice about the way she asked me. She wasn't babying me. She wasn't trying to prolong a simple question. Did I want to perform or not?

Boldly I said, "Yes, ma'am. Another chance, please."

"Well, then, let's go," the sassy coach shouted from across the room.

When the music came on this time, I nodded to Hope and Kendal, and all three of us did our thing. We had to wait a whole hour to find out if we made the team or not. The vote could have gone either way for me. I thought I did well, but I really froze up during my time to shine. I didn't know if I had what it takes.

But when the coach came out and posted the roster on the gym door, Hope screamed. Kendal screamed. They told me to look. And when I did, I screamed too. God had blessed me! I'd made the squad, even though I lacked the confidence.

Conquer Point

Confidence is tough to get just right. Either people have too much of it or folks have too little of it. To get just the right balance, remember that through the Lord you can move mountains. So be confident. He is with you always, even unto the end of the earth.

Prayer

Lord, today was a hard day. I doubted myself so much. I felt like I'd failed before I even tried. What's up with that? HELP!!! Help me get stronger and realize that I am somebody because You made me, and You never make junk. I need the Holy Spirit to guide me.

In Jesus' name, amen.

u Journal

CHAPTER 5:

may

Hoped for Change

Okay, I admit it. I'm not perfect, but I have severe friend drama. They have more problems than a math exam. Can you feel what I'm sayin' here? I want someone to listen.

Stay with the pages and ~~see if~~ anyone does.

[CHAPTER 5]

Hoped for Change

I couldn't believe I'd let Kendal talk me into studying with her again. I thought for sure that this time we would actually crack open a book and dig in, but here we were in my kitchen at the island, loading up hot dogs and hamburgers that my mom had grilled. The spread was massive: lettuce, tomatoes, onion, relish, ketchup, Dijon mustard, fries, onion rings, chips, and ice cream sundaes for dessert. My mom was so great. We did love all the food, but once again I was not studying.

After we ate more food than I had in the past two days, I tried to talk to Kendal about the math concepts that had stumped me. Now that we were getting ready for the big exam in a week or two, I wanted to make sure I passed on all the information I had gathered from my extra study time, but she wasn't into hearing me. She was admiring my laundry room and talking about the pictures on our wall. She even loved our refrigerator size. I mean, enough was enough, so I finally said something to her.

"Kendal, I love hanging out with you, but it's like you don't take schoolwork seriously. Believe me, I know how easy it is to avoid things that are hard. I've been avoiding this stuff for half a year, but both of us had better get our acts together and really study. There will be no more time to catch up. Do you get that?"

"Look, Faith, we'll have plenty of time for that. I'm not even thinking about schoolbooks. Look at you! You live in this huge house. Your dad is a star, and that's nothing to you. The closest I've ever been to a star's home was when I watched MTV cribs. I'm not saying I want my mom to be rich and famous. It'd be nice, but let's get real. So can I at least be excited? Can I enjoy it? I'm not even a Christian, and I'm pumped that I am over at Jack Tyler Thomas' house! I'm eating off his plates!"

Okay, I had to take a step back. I had to take a deep breath and look at things from her point of view. This life of mine was ordinary to me, and I couldn't act like it wasn't extraordinary for her. It wasn't major to Nellie because she lived right down the street. Kendal told me how she and her mom shared a trailer. I'd never been there. It wasn't that I had any problems with it, but I hadn't been invited. I could only imagine how different their lifestyle was from mine. Maybe I needed to understand that Kendal should be a hangout friend but not a study partner. She was too distracted to improve her grades, and her distraction was going to keep me on the F track. I had to say it straight.

> " **Look** at you! You live in this **huge** house. Your dad is **a star**, and that's **nothing** to you. "

"Kendal, this just isn't going to work for me. It's hard enough having to go through this stuff once. Do you really want to go through it twice?"

"Well, for your information, many people have to repeat stuff. That doesn't make them bad people."

"I'm not saying it does, but you have the skills to master it *this* time. Quit being such a lazy bum. Open up the notebook, and let's move on."

"Okay, okay, let me just tell you," she said, placing her hands on my shoulder after standing up in front of me as though she had some big announcement. "Naw, I can't tell you."

"What?" I said standing up beside her. She had my interest. She had to spill the beans. "Tell me, Kendal. What?"

"A girl who lives next door to me has the exam from last year. She told me the teacher never changes it. I didn't feel right not sharing it with you, so if you want we can stop wasting time, memorize the answers, and ensure ourselves a great grade."

"That's just about the dumbest thing I've ever heard in my life," I said to her. "You're going to get caught. You never made an A this whole year. You think the teacher's not going to know something is up when you suddenly ace the exam?"

"I've been forging notes from my mom to the teacher, letting her know how hard I've been

BEHIND THE SCENES
ON KENDAL

FULL NAME: Kendal Jessica Monroe
BIRTH DATE: May 1
FAMILY MAKEUP: Mom
FAVORITE COLOR: Red
FAVORITE FOOD: Chicken fingers
HOBBIES: Cheerleading and dancing
GOALS: Wants to pass algebra.
STRENGTHS: Not much gets her down.
WEAKNESS: Looks for the easy way out
ONE POSITIVE ABOUT THIS CHARACTER: Fun spirit
WORD OF INFLUENCE: Conquer
FAVORITE PHRASE: Get it done by any means necessary.

studying and working, and you probably noticed how I've been volunteering answers in class."

I had noticed. "How are you doing that?"

"I ask Jim, who sits beside me, what the answer is, and I raise my hand and say it. She already said she thinks I'm improving greatly. Let me get it from my bag and show you how simple this will be for us to do."

When she walked over to pull the test out of her bag, I felt a lump in my throat. This was a lot to process. Before she showed it to me, I felt the Holy Spirit working inside of me. I had a conscience. There was no way I was going to cheat. I might not make an A on my own, but I certainly wasn't going to make one cheating.

"It's not cool, Kendal. Cheating will cause serious problems far worse than a bad grade will. It isn't worth it." I hated the idea of that test even being near me. Who wants the temptation? As low as I felt about my recent bad grades, I knew that cheating would cause me to doubt more than my math ability—I'd doubt my integrity. I didn't want Kendal to go down that path. "Please don't."

"I'm not gonna get caught unless someone blabs. You won't rat on me, will you? You're probably required to tattle on people because of your faith and all."

"Kendal, I'm not going to rat you out. The truth is that if you miraculously have fabulous grades, you will rat yourself out. And you will have sold out. But I'm really going to hope that you will change your mind."

"Huh! Don't count on it." She looked away for a moment and then patted her stomach, ready to change the topic. "Are there any more of those chips?"

We got through our awkward moment. I knew I couldn't control what Kendal did next, but I had peace about how I had handled it. I totally understood her desperation, but she had a choice as to how she would handle it. Good friends are supposed to let each other know when what they're doing is wrong. My conscience was clear.

May was such a wonderful time of year. It wasn't too hot, and it wasn't too cold. Nashville was ideal in the spring. Nellie and I were walking together. Neither of us wanted to full-on exercise. She wasn't into it at all, and I got enough of it in cheerleading. We did it to spend time together. It was as if the walking made it easier for us to open up to one another and to get past the hard talks we'd had a couple months ago. Things were going much better between me and her.

That is until she said, "I think that soon I'm going to tell my mom that I'll be staying overnight with you."

"That'd be fun," I said. "We could do an all-night movie…"

Nellie held up her hand to interrupt me. "No, Faith. I wouldn't really stay with you. I'd be out with Ethan," she said, and then in case I wasn't getting it, she added, "at a hotel."

I know what I **thought** she said, but that couldn't be what she **actually** meant. So I said, "Are you crazy?"

"Don't get dramatic, Faith. You and I talked about this, and we don't need to revisit how you feel. I do know it's a lot to ask, and hopefully my mom won't even call so you won't have to cover for me at all. I knew I'd better have all my stuff in place. Even if you disagree with what I am doing, don't you want to help me make it special?"

She was crazy. Everything I wanted to say would have made her mad, and I hated to cause distance between us when she was facing such serious decisions. But what could I say to my friend? She was going to be intimate with someone she hadn't even known that long, and she wasn't even planning to do it God's way, which was just crazy to me! As much as I hated to tick her off, my conscience was too strong about this. I'd have to risk our friendship and tell her the truth.

"You'd want it to be special for me, right?"

She knew deep down what I thought, and she didn't really want to hear my response. I was silent. We hadn't agreed to be accountability partners or anything like that, but we were sisters in Christ. Back when I didn't know God, she went on and on telling me how great my life would be if I opened up my heart to Him. Now that she was walking away from God's plan for her life, I couldn't leave her. I had to help turn her back toward God's best for her.

"Okay, Nellie. Let's just stop walking for a second, okay. Do you really want to know what I think?"

"You don't approve of it. I got that part. But what about supporting a friend who is choosing to do something that is important to her? Isn't that friendship too?"

> "Now that **she** was **walking away** from **God's plan** for her life, I couldn't **leave** her."

"Nellie, come on. If you want me to share what's in my heart, you can't get upset. You've got to completely hear me out."

"Okay, fine. I'm listening."

I grabbed both of her hands, looked her in the eyes, and said, "There are so many reasons why I don't want you to carry out this plan of yours. I understand you're saying that this guy makes you feel things you've never felt before and you want to keep exploring all of that. You think he's cute, and he has deep feelings for you. I'm human too, and I understand wanting to be loved. But you could get pregnant or far worse! You don't know if he's a virgin or not. You might contract a disease. Both of your parents would find out, and you'd be grounded forever!"

"I thought through all of that, and I've taken proper precautions to adequately plan so that nothing like that happens, okay?"

"Well, there's something even bigger than that, Nellie. How about letting God down? Is that what you want to do?"

"God gave me these feelings, Faith. I've been talking to Him about it. Ethan's a Christian too, and we plan to pray before we do it. See, we got all that covered. The Lord

Value Verse

"You did not choose me, but I chose you and appointed you to go and bear fruit—fruit that will last."

[John 15:16]

[blog]

>>

When I need God's help, I just fall on my knees and ask for it. Unlike my friends, He always answers my call.

<<

Heather | Greenwich, CT | 13 years old | 7th Grade

---

knows how much I love Ethan. I already feel like I'm married to him. I know that sounds crazy to you, and you can't relate, but it's true! Nothing is going to stop me from making this happen, and if you don't want to cover for me, I'll find another way."

I didn't feel comfortable covering for her, but I wasn't ready to end our dialogue. I was afraid that I was the only person Nellie was confiding in right now. I might be the only person to encourage her to change her mind. "I've got to think about it. I'm sorry, but I just can't say that I'm going to lie for you."

"I'd be there for you."

> " It was **all good**. My only confusion was about those **weird feelings** for Niles. "

"Well, if my needing time to think about it isn't a good enough answer for you, then do whatever."

"Okay, okay. I'll give you more time to think about it, but just know that I'm counting on my best friend to help me out here. I want to share this with you. I'll always remember my first time, and I want it to be so special, Faith."

I didn't want her sharing any of that with me. What she had already told me was way too much info. I could only hope her mind wasn't completely made up about this, but by the way she was talking, a change of heart seemed impossible.

I was so happy when all of my exams were over. I felt pretty good about everything, even science and algebra. My life wasn't so bad. My parents were still happy. My mom's business was growing. My dad had finished his album, and it was going to drop in June. I hadn't seen much of Joy or Blake, which sometimes was a good thing. I'd made the cheerleading squad at school, and I was growing in my faith. It was all good. My only confusion was about those weird feelings for Niles. Even so, I'd wanted my life to be better…and it was.

Mother's Day was even good. My grandmother came up for dinner and brought my sweet little cousin Belle. When my mom and grandmother talked alone, I could tell something wasn't great with my aunt, but I didn't listen or ask questions. I just enjoyed my cousin and was happy to let the two mother-figures in my life know how much they meant to me. Yep! The month of May was great for me. I was learning to appreciate all my blessings. It felt uplifting to be full and to appreciate the good stuff.

After a long day of playing with a five-year-old, I was exhausted. I was ready for bed and looking forward to a deep sleep when my phone rang. I looked at the caller ID and saw it

> I used to hurt so badly that I'd ask God why, what have I done to deserve any of this? I feel now He was preparing me for this, for the future. That's the way I see it.
>
> — JANET JACKSON

HOLIDAYS

Cinco de Mayo → May 5
Mother's Day → May 13
Memorial Day → May 28

HAPPY BIRTHDAY TO YOU

Janet Jackson → May 16

SOMETHING TO DO

Go out for Mexican food with a friend and remind them how special they are to you.

THINK ABOUT IT

You were put on the earth for a reason. Ask God to begin to reveal to you His purposes for your life.

HISTORY LESSON

On May 5, 1862, 4000 Mexican soldiers were victorious over the French and traitor Mexican armies at Puebla, Mexico. This day is celebrated as Cinco de Mayo.

Faith's Timeline

May 1st → Kendal's birthday
5th → Kendal reveals she plans to cheat on her exam. Crazy!
12th → Nellie says she will lose her virginity. Sad!
25th → Hope plans to run away! Scary!
30th → Praying hard for my three dear friends and for me as well. We're all crazy.
Mondays, Wednesdays, Saturdays: cheer practice

was Hope. I picked it up and started to say hello, but she began to ramble. I couldn't make out anything she was saying for the first few seconds.

"Hope, you've gotta talk to me. I mean you've gotta talk to me so that I can understand you," I said, sitting up in my bed. I wanted to have a clear head. My friend needed her accountability partner. I just prayed while she calmed herself down. **Lord, give me the strength to help Hope. I don't know what's going on with her, but obviously it's something big. Just talk through me. In Jesus' name, amen.**

"Do you hear me?" she asked. "I should let you go to sleep. You're tired."

"No, Hope. Please don't hang up. I was praying. Okay? I'm listening. I'm awake and ready. Talk to me."

"I'll just run away. My dad went off on me and took his stupid wife's side of an argument. I'm just going to pack up my stuff and get the heck away from here. It's like she's always picking on me and messing with me. My sister doesn't get treated this way. She never tells Holly to clean up. Then she's going to try to throw in my face that my dad shouldn't do this or that for me because 'I won't do anything for him.' I hate that he's on the road so much. You can understand that, can't you? It's like when he's away, she turns into the evil stepmother. I'm not exaggerating, Faith. She's crazy!"

"Hope, what is running away going to accomplish? Where are you going to go?"

"Well, I've got money. I can take it out of the bank, and the people I performed with last summer asked me to sing background with them. My dad said I'm too young, but I can catch up with them. I can find out where they are, sing with them, and make some money."

"What about school, Hope?"

Conquer Point

Sometimes you will be the only one in your group who plans to stand for God. Don't let your friends sway you to fall to temptation. Instead, pray your friends through their crises. The God you serve can change the hearts of any person, just like He changed you.

"I'm quitting school. I don't need it. I see how much money my dad brings in, and he didn't go to college."

"Yeah, but he finished high school."

"You don't get it, Faith. You're not any help!" She sounded so frantic, it scared me a little.

"Hope, have you ever spoken to your stepmom one-on-one? Maybe she would be supportive of who you are if you gave her a chance to know you. I adore you because I know you. And maybe it's the same with your dad. He should know his daughter and have a heart bigger than the circumstances right now, but maybe he hasn't had the chance to be a good father because you won't let him make it right."

Hope was crying loudly at this point. "Your life is great, Faith. You really don't understand what it feels like to be heartbroken in your own home."

"Hope, you know my family has had hard times. I told you about them."

"But you guys work through it. We all ignore one another. It's hopeless." With that, she hung up, and I knew it was useless to call her back. Even though she had faith, she was lost in her sadness. I prayed that she just needed time.

I was so frustrated. I couldn't connect with any of my friends. I couldn't get through to them. I couldn't get them to see what I could see clearly. I was allowing the Holy Spirit to work in me to help them, but it wasn't easy. They needed to bring their stuff to God and let **Him** show them the way. Hope wanted me to say running away was okay. Nellie wanted me to act like any choice she made was okay just because she was a Christian. Kendal wanted to pretend that bad choices were fine as long as they took you to where you wanted to go.

Again, I wasn't perfect, but I was learning how to take everything to God.

With my friends hurting, I felt like I was off track too. As pleased as I was with my life at that moment, my friends needed the power of prayer big time. They were my friends, and when they hurt, I hurt. So I got down on my knees and went to God in prayer. I wasn't at peace. I was worried for my friends. I could only do one thing—for each of them I hoped for change.

Prayer

Lord, today I am praying an unselfish prayer. I need You to show my friends Your way and Your love. They are losing it. They want to do everything but the right things. And hanging around them is taking so much from me. Can You fill us all with Your love? I am hoping and praying and believing for a miracle. Thanks in advance. I feel better resting in Your grace.

In Jesus' name, amen.

CHAPTER 6:

june

Stressed-Out Completely

Have you ever had one of those days when you just wondered if things will ever get better? I feel like the wind won't stop blowing trouble my way. People tell me I've got it going on, but inside I feel like I have nothing together. I'm sitting still, but I'm so jittery. I want things to calm down. *Will they?*

[CHAPTER 6]
Stressed-Out Completely

Usually I could gain a moment of serenity by spending time alone beside the pool in our backyard. However, today was very different. I was stressing myself out. As my long hair moved around my face in the occasional breeze, my worries were swirling around my mind. I hadn't talked to Kendal, Hope, or Nellie, and visions of everything that could go wrong in their circumstances popped into my mind. I wanted to reach out to Kendal so bad, but I knew she wouldn't be open to my comments or opinions. She actually cheated on the test! If the teacher had caught her, Kendal could have been suspended for the first few days of the next school year. And she'd never get to stay on the cheerleading squad. I didn't know what to do except keep praying for her.

There were thoughts of Nellie. What if she did get pregnant? She said she was taking care of everything by using protection, but that was a worldly version of security. Nothing would protect her heart and her soul and her life the way God's wholeness could. What if she is heartbroken because of her choice? *Maybe I should call*, I thought. *Maybe Nellie is too proud to call me and ask for a shoulder to cry on or a listening ear.* But my pride wouldn't let me call her because in my mind I could hear her either yelling at me for not supporting her or telling me all the details. I couldn't handle either conversation. All I could do was pray for her as well.

And then there was Hope. What if she changed her mind but didn't have enough money to get home? Maybe she would try to call me, but her cell phone wouldn't work. But Hope could easily find a way to call me if she wanted to talk. I had to believe that she would be okay and that she would come to her senses.

My head hurt. All this worrying in such a short time. I was letting my mind get the best of me. As I gritted my teeth, I felt something touch my shoulder. I was startled and instinctively grabbed a rock near me. I was ready to protect myself. Niles laughed.

"Whoa, there! You don't play games, do you? Please don't hit me." He pretended to be scared.

I hid my smile and tried to talk quickly to also hide my embarrassment. "I don't play games, but it seems like everyone else does. You need to announce yourself next time. Are you crazy, scaring me like that?"

"I'm sorry. I was walking by and saw someone out here. From a distance it looked like you, so I took my chances. I want to talk. You got a sec?"

Now my heart was racing for a different reason. The guy standing before me made me so nervous. He was sort of shy but also confident. It was a strange and likeable combination. Did I have a second? Did I want to talk? Honestly, I didn't want him to leave. I wondered what it was that he came to say.

"Have you heard of using the phone?" I didn't want to make it too easy for him.

"Is that a no?"

"Well, since you are here, and you did risk possible death by sunblock, you might as well have a seat." I motioned beside me and he sat down.

Squinting in the sun, I watched Niles swipe his bangs to the side a couple times. I could tell it was a nervous habit. Then he spoke with surprising confidence. "I just want to be honest with you, is that okay? I know most of our friends play games, but that isn't my thing. Maybe it would be, but I'm not any good at it. So here it goes." He rubbed his hands together as if warming them.

I nodded and smiled. I wanted him to feel comfortable telling me what his true feelings were. We were friends. No need to have unclear stuff between us. But when he reached out and grabbed my hand, his touch took my breath away.

"I really like you, Faith. I find myself thinking about you when I wake up in the morning. I make sure I run into you in the hallways at school. You've probably noticed that by now." Niles gave a small, self-conscious laugh, as though he couldn't believe he was saying this to me.

That made two of us.

It had seemed like he was around me at school a lot more, but I thought it was because I was sort of interested in him. It never fails that as soon as you have a bit of a crush on a guy, you become hyperaware of his whereabouts at all times.

Niles continued. "I know your routine. Now that school's out, I won't be able to see you as easily. I figured I'd better express what I'm feeling and see if you have any feelings for me. I want to see if maybe you want to act on this."

"Act on it?" I said, being caught off guard a little. I mean, what kind of girl did he think I was? I wondered if he knew what was going on with his sister. If he did know, he'd also better know I would make a very different choice.

"I was thinking we could date. Maybe date exclusively. That is, if you think I'm cool an' all. I sort of think you do."

"What do you mean?" I said, wondering how he was coming up with his rationale about my feelings for him.

"You ask a lot of questions. Kinda puts a guy on the spot, you know? I didn't mean that you thought I was the greatest guy to ever live…all I meant was that it seems like we have a connection. When we've been around one another, I've felt like you get me and maybe want to know me the way I want to know you. You smile at me like no other girl ever has. We almost speak to each other without even saying a word. I've never had that

> **Value Verse**
>
> "We know that in all things God works for the good of those who love him, who have been called according to his purpose. For those God foreknew he also predestined to be conformed to the likeness of his Son, that he might be the firstborn among many brothers. And those he predestined, he also called; those he called, he also justified; those he justified, he also glorified."
>
> [Romans 8:28–30]

kind of connection. Girls who don't care about a guy also don't get so flustered around him. I think I make you a little nervous, and I want to change that. I want you to be comfortable. I want us to be able to share stuff. I want us to be close." Niles paused a second before continuing. "What are you thinking? I can't read your expression very well."

> "I really **like** you, **Faith**. I find myself thinking about you when I **wake up** in the morning."

He surprised me. This was too fast. I had just gotten used to the idea that I might sort of like a guy, so I said the only thing I thought I could say in a situation like this. "I just want to be friends. I'm not ready for anything else. Sorry if I misled you."

I got up and dashed into our house through the French doors, leaving Niles a bit flustered and completely alone with my rejection. I felt bad about what I had said to him, but it had to be done. I had to end whatever we had before it really got started, but as he pointed out, it had already begun. Yeah, it was the right thing to do. I hoped.

Once in the house, I saw my mom sitting in the great room. She was pulling at her bangs like she does when she is stressed. **Kinda like Niles**, I thought. I stopped dwelling on my problems and asked, "Mom, what's wrong?"

"Oh, sweetie, it's nothing. Just stuff Mom's got to handle." She turned away.

"Mom," I said, "please tell me."

"I just want to get some girls in the pageant, Faith, and the girls who want to be in it are not fully committed. I don't want to enter someone who isn't ready to step up to this with confidence. The girls who could handle the challenge are busy with other obligations. Well, all except for this one girl who won't do it."

I knew she was talking about me. How could I not help out her talent agency?

"I'll do it, Mom," I said, without letting any negative thoughts take over.

Her eyes lit up like fire. "Faith baby, thank you. Today is the last day to enter potential contestants. I must do that right now. We'll start planning after that, okay?"

Only after I heard her drive off did the flood of self-doubt begin. **What did I just commit to?**

A week later I was standing at attention with other pageant entrants. Mrs. Knight, a petite lady with glasses resting on the end of her nose, was sizing every girl up and down. She had two ladies helping her. I saw them analyzing me as they walked by. Poor Mom. She placed her hope in me, and I was probably going to get thrown out first.

When the women got to the last girl and made some final notes, Mrs. Knight went to the very front of the posh hotel banquet room and addressed all of us. "Welcome, ladies. I need you all to introduce yourselves. We take the Miss Teen Nashville pageant very seriously. The winner will represent our great city in the state pageant. The winner of the state pageant will, of course, go on to represent Tennessee in the Miss Teen USA contest. It is an honor just to be here today. For those fortunate enough to go on and compete for Miss Teen Nashville, you share in a legacy with women of great accomplishment."

Mrs. Knight looked over her glasses as if cueing us to applaud. So we did. I had to admit, I had a few chills go up and down my spine.

JUNE

SOMETHING TO DO

Have a summer tea and invite your friends over. Take lots of pictures to go in your summer scrapbook. Create fun iced teas by adding cranberry or other fruit juices and don't forget a festive, summer touch with little umbrellas placed in each.

HOLIDAYS

Flag Day → June 14

HAPPY BIRTHDAY TO YOU

Kanye West → June 8
Natalie Portman → June 9
Paula Abdul → June 19
Prince William → June 21
Author Stephanie Perry Moore → June 28

THINK ABOUT IT

When was the last time you read your Bible? Pick it up, find a new verse, and memorize it.

HISTORY LESSON

On June 27, 1898, Joshua Slocum became the first person to successfully circumnavigate the earth alone when he landed his boat, the "Spray", in Newport, Rhode Island. His trip was a total of 46,000 miles long.

I think it's very important that you make your own decision about what you are. Therefore you're responsible for your actions, so you don't blame other people.

PRINCE WILLIAM

[blog]

>>

When I get stressed, I turn on the Christian station. Whatever is playing blesses my soul and calms me down.

<<

Lacey | Boca Raton, FL | 12 years old | 6th Grade

One by one, the other girls presented themselves like they'd been doing it since birth.

"Hi! I'm Jillian. I'm 15, and I've entered this pageant to win. Look out, girls!"

There's nothing wrong with confidence, but she was over the top. Mrs. Knight called on me to go after her, and, of course, I was very nervous. My body was shaking all over as I said, "I'm Faith Thomas. I'm 14 years old and…"

I couldn't say that I was happy to be there because that wouldn't be true, and I couldn't say that I hoped I'd win because that sounded too bold for how I was feeling. I didn't know what to say, so I just kept saying "and" like a stuck robot.

"Yes, fine…" Mrs. Knight referred to her notes to check my name. "Miss Thomas, thank you for being here. You'll want to brush up on your presentation skills, darling."

Uh, ya think?

The tea that followed the presentations was set up so all the girls could meet and greet one another. It wasn't competition time yet. Jillian was hanging out with this other cute girl. Jillian's teased blonde hair was so bouncy and pageant-like. When I looked at her friend, she looked at me in return and began whispering something to Jillian. That made me frustrated. *I can't believe they're talking about me!* Someone walked up beside me.

"They're just jealous," a cool voice said. I turned to see Holly, Hope's sister. I was stunned for two reasons: She was being nice to me and she was here entering a beauty pageant. This was exactly the kind of thing I figured she would mock me about. She was into her basketball and her tough-girl attitude.

"Don't look all weird like that. Basketball players are beautiful too."

"You're gorgeous. I'm just—"

"Girl, pick your mouth up off the ground."

"Hey, what's the word on Hope? I've been so worried about her."

Holly nodded. "That's good of you. She's fine. She was gone about half a day when Dad found out and went after her. She was still waiting at the bus station, thank goodness. They had a long talk and Hope came home. Things actually seem better. But you know how strange families are."

"I do know."

Holly turned to glare at Jillian and the other girl until they stopped talking. To me she said, "Don't worry about those two over there. They're the kind who like to intimidate others, but the truth is that you're intimidating them."

> "Flat out **serious**. Faith, you're a **winner**. I know it, and you can **bet** they **know** it."

"You're making fun of me, aren't you?"

"No. Flat out serious. Faith, you're a winner. I know it, and you can bet they know it. I like watchin' them squirm. This could be a very fun pageant."

I wanted to give her a hug for saying such nice things to me, but she wasn't that type of girl. When I really thought about it, I had just as good a chance as those two girls did. My mom and even Holly had confidence in me. It was about time that I had confidence in myself.

Getting ready to go on tour with my father was so frustrating. Everyone was scrambling around the house to make our departure time. My father wasn't happy about the fact that we were off schedule before the tour even began!

"Lily, why aren't the bags down in the foyer yet?" My father said, trying to control his impatience.

"Jack, I don't know. I'm sorry. Time has just gotten away from us."

"I need y'all to hurry. I asked the band to be there at a certain time, and I don't want to be the one who's holding everyone up. With our first performance tonight, we can't miss our plane to New York."

My mother was usually on top of stuff like this. She never mismanaged time, but she'd been really busy with her agency work. I sort of went with the flow, but Joy and Blake and even Dad seemed to always be griping about Mom's work taking over. I thought maybe Dad was forgetting how often his work took him away from us for long periods of time.

After Mom apologized, Dad's mood was diffused and we all worked together to get out the door. Even Joy was offering to help carry suitcases out, which was more than a miracle. We were showing godly character to one another and that was great. I think God honored that because in less than two hours we were on the plane headed to New York City. I hadn't ever been with my father on the plane. I had only toured with him on a bus. It was something special to me to be sitting in first class. It was so cool. I looked around to see what other people on board were doing to enjoy the first-class style. Some people were dining on steak, others sipped champagne, and a few folks were sleeping like babies in the roomy seats.

As I scanned the room, my eyes focused on someone who was looking at me. The drummer! Every time I assured myself I must be imagining his stares, I turned around and sure enough, he was looking intensely at me. When he winked at me, I pretended not to notice, and I focused my attention on the movie. Thankfully I didn't have much longer to be worried about Drew because we landed 20 minutes later and were ushered into limousines almost immediately. We were taken to the Tabernacle Church, which was a beautiful facility. It was cozy and quaint, yet it could seat almost 5000 people. Just being in the place made me think of how I would love to worship God in such a building.

That night the packed house loved my father's performance. Before we knew it, the show was over. We stayed at the W hotel not too far away. The hospitality suite was decked out with food, and people from the church came over to meet my father. He prayed with his band before going out into the lounge area to meet his guests. My mother asked me if I was coming with her, but I needed to use the ladies' room first. I told her I'd be there in a sec.

"Not too long, hon. You know how your dad likes everyone to meet his family."

Checking myself out in the bathroom mirror was a mistake. I didn't have a comb, so I finger-combed my hair. I looked like a wild child. My mouth felt yucky, and I didn't have any toothpaste, so I gargled a little with water. When I opened the door to leave, I was startled to see Drew waiting outside the door.

"Well, don't you look lovely?" He said as he touched my face and slid his hands down to my shoulders. "What was taking you so long? Were you checking yourself out in the mirror? You're beautiful, darling. I can tell you were checking me out on the plane. I just knew that you wanted some time alone with me."

Panic filled me. I stepped back and kept thinking, "Scream, scream for help. Tell him to back off!" But I couldn't say anything. My lack of self-esteem made me clam up. I wanted him to take his hands off of me! I kept stepping back until I ended up in the ladies' room again. He followed me in and turned off the lights. It was so dark! I could feel him breathing on me. What was he going to do to me? Why was I so passive? Why didn't I scream and call out for help? As I felt him place his other hand on my shoulder, I began to cry. I was stressed out completely.

Conquer Point

Take a deep breath. Count to ten. Things are going to get better. There's no need to worry when you know the One who is in control. And though sometimes it may feel like He has abandoned you, rest assured. Stop stressing. God's got you.

Prayer

Jesus, the waves keep on raging in my life. It's hard to tell which end is up. I'm trying to find hope within so that I can know You'll lead me through, but I'm having a hard time dealin'. Rescue me, please. Amen.

SELF-ESTEEM GROWS

Why Am I Here?

You were put here for a reason. You weren't just a random thought in the universe. God knew you before He hung the first star in the sky. "You did not choose me, but I chose you and appointed you to go and bear fruit—fruit that will last" (John 15:16). You are important to God because He wants to work through you to reach others who are lost. He knows exactly what He wants you to do, and He knows exactly the path He wants you to take. But you never know how God is going to work, so just go with His flow and don't try to take control. "For my thoughts are not your thoughts, neither are your ways my ways" (Isaiah 55:8).

Believe me, there is nowhere you can take yourself that is better than where God wants to take you. "'For I know the plans I have for you,' declares the LORD, 'plans to prosper you and not to harm you'" (Jeremiah 29:11). Remember that your life has meaning because God has given you a purpose. Live your life in constant fulfillment of that purpose, and all your days will be blessed of the Lord and full of peace and joy.

[self-esteem quiz]

Poise or Poison? Which do you choose?

[Jeremiah 29:11; Jeremiah 1:5; Philippians 4:8; Philippians 4:13]

Poise — *noun*	Poison — *noun*
1) Being balanced, stable, real	1) Something destructive or fatal
2) Knowing who you are and who you are not	2) Something that has an inhibiting or harmful influence
3) A calm, confident state of mind	3) Something that pollutes

1 >> When you are about to try something new, do you
   a) *Try to find a way out*
   b) *Think of all the reasons you can't do it and end up failing*
   c) *Learn all you can and try your best*

2 >> If you walk into a room and people quit talking, do you
   a) *Quietly walk back out, sure they were talking about you*
   b) *Find a friendly face in the room and stay close to that person*
   c) *Barely notice and join in the group*

3 >> The newest fashion trend in school just doesn't look good on you. Do you
   a) *Decide the way you look is beyond hope and dress to disappear*
   b) *Wear it anyway so you can fit in*
   c) *Change it up a little so it looks good on you*

4 >> When you look in a mirror, do you
   a) *Truly dislike the person you see*
   b) *Wish you could be someone else*
   c) *See good and bad and decide to make the best of what you've got*

5 >> When you meet someone for the first time, do you see
   a) *A potential critic*
   b) *A stranger*
   c) *A potential friend*

6 >> A new girl moves into your neighborhood. Do you
   a) *Decide she wouldn't like you even before you meet her*
   b) *Walk by her house hoping she'll speak to you*
   c) *Invite her to your house and introduce her to your friends*

7. >> Which of these sounds like the most fun?
   a) *Stay home and watch a movie*
   b) *Invite a friend to spend the night*
   c) *Have a slumber party and experiment with hair and makeup*

8. >> Which answer best fits the way you feel most of the time?
   a) *Life is difficult and lonely*
   b) *Life is like a roller coaster, full of ups and downs*
   c) *Life is an adventure full of discovery and joy*

9. >> Which word best describes the way you view yourself?
   a) *Unacceptable*
   b) *Insecure*
   c) *Hopeful*

10. >> Which statement is most true of you?
   a) *I really have nothing to offer*
   b) *I have a few good qualities*
   c) *I am the best me I know how to be*

[quiz results]

Give yourself one point for each "a," two points for each "b," and three points for each "c."

If you scored 10–15
You have been told lies about yourself and have believed them. People, events, and circumstances can sometimes send us negative messages that we can either choose to believe or refuse to accept. If we accept these messages they become like poison, polluting our thoughts and destroying our lives. Did you know that the Bible says that God knew you before you were ever born? Did you know He has a good future and a life full of purpose chosen just for you? Fill your mind with God's truth, and stop believing the lies that keep you from walking in the poise and promise God wants for you.

If you scored 16–24
You are only beginning to see all that you might become. You see some good things about yourself, but you are afraid the rest of the world will not agree. Some days you find yourself thinking poisonous thoughts about yourself, and some days you find poise to be in you. The only difference is what you choose to believe. When the poison-filled thoughts come, refuse to listen. Don't let destructive thoughts keep you from being all that God wants you to be.

If you scored 25–30
You are headed for a life of adventure and discovery! You know who you are and do not allow poison thinking to infect your life. You face life with poise and confidence and never think to run away. Just remember that your confidence should always be in the one thing that remains unchanging—God and His love for you. A woman who knows who she is and who God is will always walk with poise and strength.

CHAPTER 7:

july

Surprised by Confidence

The breaking point, you know that point in time, that place in your life, when you feel like you cannot be held accountable for your actions because you can't take it anymore? The place where you blow your top if any pettiness comes your way? The place where everyone had better come at you the right way or they'd better not step up to you at all? Well, if that place sounds familiar to you...watch out...

that's where I am.

[CHAPTER 7]

Surprised *by* Confidence

My instincts kicked in when Drew tried to attack me. As he moved to my left, I moved to the right and dashed for the swinging bathroom door and out to the hallway. My eyes scanned up and down the corridor, and standing near the elevator and just a couple yards from me was Blake. He could tell by my look of fear that something was wrong. Immediately, I ran behind him. He stretched out his arms to protect me. I didn't think anything about him being younger than me. Blake's confidence and his look of stern strength made me believe he really could shield me from Drew.

"What are you doing to my sister?" Blake yelled.

"Oh, don't get all worked up, little man. We're hanging out. Your dad asked me to check on her. Jack likes to be surrounded by his good-looking family when the cameras are flashing."

> **" I glanced around to see which way Blake and I should run if Drew came any closer. "**

I couldn't believe he was dismissing his sinful actions. Who knows what would have happened if I would have stayed in that dark bathroom with him another few seconds? My legs felt like Jell-O.

"I find that interesting because Dad just asked me to come and find Faith. Don't lie, Drew."

With his rugged voice, Drew continued. "I was just telling your sister how pretty she is. Don't you think she's pretty?" He walked a few more feet until we were all standing close together. I glanced around to see which way Blake and I should run if Drew came any closer.

I couldn't believe he had the guts to step toward me to try to touch my hair. My brother quickly hit his hand away. I wanted to say something to him. I wanted to speak up for myself and let him know to never touch me again, but I was trapped in my shield of insecurity. *I must have done something to allow him to think he could touch me like that.*

The smug look Drew had on his face was sickening, like he felt he'd won. I'm sure he knew there was nothing I could do to prove what he had done. He'd stepped over the line with me, but my silence made him believe his secret was safe.

My brother broke the silence and said, "Leave my sister alone. Don't speak or look at her. If I catch you cornering her again, I'll—"

"What're you gonna do, little man?" Drew said with a mocking tone, laughing at us both.

"Don't even try to mess with me. And you know you're gonna have to pay big time when Dad gets here."

Drew laughed, but he started to head the opposite direction. He waved his hand at us like we were not worth bothering with.

I dropped to the floor and put my hands to my face. I let out loud sobs.

"I'm gonna get Mom and Dad," Blake said.

"No, don't leave. What are we going to say?" I sobbed even louder.

"They need to know and that guy needs to be gone. I may be in elementary school, Faith, but I'm on hall patrol and we watched movies about this in training—adults aren't allowed to mess with kids! Our parents really need to know. Besides, don't forget my name is Rock. I won't let that guy hurt you, Faith."

"Just don't leave, Blake. Please." I could barely make out those words. I wanted to run in search of my parents, but I knew my legs wouldn't move.

Blake bit his bottom lip and looked down the hall. "I won't leave. I'll just walk to the hall intersection and call out for them. Okay?" He patted me on the back.

I looked up and him and nodded.

How was I going to explain this to my mother, let alone my father? Every time I came around he ended up having to fire someone. Last year there had been my dad's connection with that backup singer and I found out. The next thing I knew, she had left the band. And now this. Before I could think about what I was going to

BEHIND THE SCENES
ON BLAKE

FULL NAME: Blake (Rock) Thomas
BIRTH DATE: July 15
FAMILY MAKEUP: Dad, Mom, and big sisters Faith and Joy
FAVORITE COLOR: Blue
FAVORITE FOOD: Hot wings
HOBBIES: Baseball
GOALS: To be a professional baseball player. To keep a clean room so Mom won't fuss.
STRENGTHS: Really smart
WEAKNESS: Doesn't always stand up for himself
ONE POSITIVE ABOUT THIS CHARACTER: Very protective of his sisters
WORD OF INFLUENCE: Go
FAVORITE PHRASE: No worries

say, I saw my mom, dad, and Joy running toward me.

My dad rushed over to me on the floor and helped me up. "Faith, look at me, sweetie. Blake said Drew did something to you."

"I'm okay, Dad. I'm not hurt."

"Faith." My mom came over and hugged me tight. "Honey, what did happen? We are very concerned."

Before I could respond Joy came over and said, "Sis, you want to talk to me? Did that man hurt you or something?"

I know all four of them cared so much and they were my family, but they were making too much out of this. So I snapped, "Get back, please! I'm okay!"

Joy, Blake, and Mom stepped back with surprise, but my dad moved even closer to me and said, "Listen, I want to know what happened right now! You might not think it's a big deal, but I have a problem with one of my band members getting too close to my children."

There was something different in my father's eyes. I saw a look of protection and a look of revenge. "Dad, you're scaring me."

> **"There was something different in my father's eyes. I saw a look of protection and a look of revenge."**

"Faith, just tell your father what he needs to know," Mom said. There was fear and insistence in her voice.

"I don't know. Drew kept staring at me all day. He's spoken to me in the past, but today was different. He must've seen me walk in to the restroom because he was waiting for me when I came out. Then I got scared because he touched me and was talking to me like he knew me, so I went back to the bathroom and he followed me. I got out of there as soon as I could."

"Faith, you did good, and you did nothing to cause him to act this way." My dad kissed me on the cheek. "You know that, right?"

"Yes. I think so."

My dad then stormed down the corridor. When he got to the main lounge area, we knew it because we could hear him letting Drew have it. He was firing him and telling him that the police had been called. My mom held me as I started to cry. It felt good to be taken care of, and my fear gave way to relief.

"Baby, you can't let people treat you badly and get away with things that are wrong. You're worth too much to us."

Covered with my parents' love, I was starting to understand that if I truly loved myself, then I had to act like it. I understood that it was important to speak up for myself because I was God's child, and I was worth protecting.

✳ ✳ ✳ ✳ ✳

"Faith Noel Thomas! Why in the world haven't you moved these clothes from the washing machine to the dryer?" my mom yelled as I went through the kitchen.

Her response seemed over the top for the situation. Granted, she had told us many times not to leave wet clothes sitting for long, but still. My raised eyebrows must have given away my feelings about her reaction.

"Okay. Well, if they haven't been there long, then I'm sorry."

"Mom, can I please finish my clothes later? I really want to hit the water before Blake's friends come over for his birthday party. They'll completely take over the pool."

"Just go ahead, Faith. I'll do it."

I had the French door barely open when she blew a fuse again. "Faith, you mixed your dark clothes with your white clothes! You know how to do this better. Come here! Now this load is completely blended."

I don't know what she was talking about because I put only white T-shirts in that load, but when I looked at the clothes in the washer again, I saw my brother's dark jeans in my load.

When I pointed that out to her, she apologized once again. As she bent over to examine all of the clothes, she grabbed her head as if she had a migraine headache. My mom had been taking on a lot lately.

"Mom, are you okay?" I asked while placing my hand on her back. "Is it Dad? Is it work? Do you not want me to ask?"

She got up slowly, shook her head, and said, "It's nothing, sweetie. Your mother's just trying to deal with some stuff. Go enjoy your summer."

She knew I wasn't going to go away until I was sure that she was all right. What could I do but believe that she was telling the truth? I guess I hoped that God would take care of everything that was going on with her.

The party was just a couple hours away, and I wondered if that was getting to her. I actually

Value Verse

"My grace is sufficient for you, for my power is made perfect in weakness. Therefore I will boast all the more gladly about my weaknesses, so that Christ's power may rest on me."

[Romans 8:28-30]

felt bad for Blake because even though it was his special day, Mom was having him do the pre-party cleaning and set up. When I got out to the pool, he was repositioning folding tables over by the barbeque. I took pity on him and decided to skip a swim and help him. Within 30 minutes we had all tables, chairs, and decorations set up. Joy even joined us, so we worked even faster.

When Mom stepped out to the patio to check on us, she seemed impressed with what we had accomplished. She was smiling for the first time today until Joy opened her mouth and

Surprised by Confidence | 79

asked what we were all wondering, "Why does Blake have to do everything for his own birthday? We always give the birthday person the day off. It's like he's your maid or something."

Mom's face immediately fell into a frown. No, it was a scowl. "If he wants to have a big party this afternoon, then he needs to help. That's what's wrong with men now. They all think they can do whatever they want because women will always be around to clean up after them and take care of all the necessary details. Well, I'm not raising a son like that. Blake, you will be better than that, and you will take responsibility for your actions."

All three of us looked at each other. Our mom had completely lost it. I thought it was the first time they had seen my mother snap, but after she returned to the house my brother and sister informed me that she had been doing this for a couple days. I thought about how weird she was acting in the laundry room. It was time for me to pray for her.

"Do you think that Dad's been lying again?" my sister asked.

"Let's not jump to conclusions."

"Maybe it's that time of the month!" my brother yelled out, stunning both Joy and myself. "What? I'm in the fifth grade, and we have to learn about the stuff girls go through."

> **"All three of us looked at each other. Our mom had completely lost it."**

"Please tell me you're kidding," I said.

Blake shrugged and confessed, "Well, they didn't really tell us. My buddies and I snuck in on some of their sessions."

"Blake, that's so dumb," Joy said.

"Yeah, it really is," I replied.

"Trust me. Once we found out what was going on with you girls, we wished we had never snuck in." At that, the three of us laughed. I left Joy and Blake to blow up some more balloons with the helium tank while I went to pray for Mom.

"Lord," I said, "please help her. I don't know what's going on with our mom, but You do. Please work it out for her because things seem like they're too much to bear. In Jesus' name, amen."

I could only hope that God would answer this prayer for Mom soon.

The next week did seem a little better. My mom was happier when she walked me into the first official session for the Miss Teen Nashville pageant. In fact, she was far happier and more excited than I was.

She wanted to make sure that my hair was perfect, that I smiled "properly" (whatever that meant), and that I didn't slouch while sitting in my chair. She didn't know how inadequate she made me feel by trying to fix everything about me constantly. I didn't want to disappoint her, and I didn't want her to snap again like she did on Blake's birthday, so I tolerated her gestures and hoped this would all be over soon.

When I spotted Holly across the room, I saw my chance to escape my mother's undivided attention. I said, "Mom, I'm going to talk to Hope's sister."

"Oh. You're making friends. That's great! Bye, sweetie."

When I approached Holly she waved her hand at me and asked, "You think you can come over here to speak to me?"

"Okay, let's drop the attitude," I replied with a little wave of my hand to match her move and then a shift of my hip to show her up.

"I see someone's growing a backbone. Oh,

SOMETHING TO DO

Invite your friends and family over for a cookout, and afterward watch some fireworks. If there is any tension, this is a great time to clear the air.

HOLIDAYS
Independence Day → July 4

HAPPY BIRTHDAY TO YOU
Hilarie Burton → July 1
Michelle Branch → July 2
Ryan Cabrera → July 18
James Lafferty → July 25

THINK ABOUT IT

Think about the freedoms you enjoy and be grateful to those veterans who helped protect them.

Faith's Timeline

July 2nd → Tour with family
15th → Mom is on the rampage
15th → Blake's (Rock's) birthday
19–24th → Pageant practice

> I followed my heart and figured that if I tried and failed, at least I'd know that I tried.
>
> — MICHELLE BRANCH

HISTORY LESSON

Independence Day is the celebration of America's official split from Britain's rule, and the beginning of the American Revolution.

[blog]

>>

Even when I don't always believe in myself, the Lord has faith in me. He has a plan for my life intertwined with unconditional love.

<<

Angela | Boise, ID | 14 years old | 8th Grade

snap! I guess you've been learning something. I guess you're not going to let these pageant winner wannabe's get under your skin?"

"With the luck I've had, Holly, they'd better not try me."

"Oh, yeah. You definitely can hang with me."

"Girls, places, please. We don't have time for chitchat," Mrs. Knight ordered.

It was summer and way too hot to be inside. Even with the air on full blast, we all wanted to be in a swimming pool somewhere. But we had to control ourselves and be refined young ladies. We were supposed to listen to her going on and on.

Then the session got interesting. We all got the opportunity to stand up and share something about ourselves that we didn't like. Holly and I looked at one another with raised eyebrows at that one. Somehow the idea of standing up and dissin' on yourself did not sound like an enjoyable activity. As Mrs. Knight kicked off our session with a speech about self-esteem, I couldn't believe it. I mean, I knew it was a topic I struggled with, but I was in a room with a bunch of gorgeous girls. Weren't they satisfied with themselves?

My question was answered by the time only three girls had spoken. They all had a long list of what was wrong with themselves. So I wasn't alone after all. I tried to listen to each girl as she shared her feelings, but I was also anxiously trying to think of what I would say when it was my turn to stand.

Holly looked at me and said, "This is a little surprising, don't you think? Not a one of 'em seems too satisfied."

The ones who we admired for their height stood up and said they felt like giraffes. The ones who were naturally slim and petite and who we all knew would look great in a bathing suit, stood up and said they felt self-conscious and too thin. The girls with enviable curves felt they were too chunky.

Some didn't like the color or texture of their hair. Others had skin color issues. I was actually surprised when Holly stood up and said that she wished she had a little more color.

"I don't know why black girls trip on me. They think I'm all that because I'm light-skinned. Then white girls say I don't fit in because I'm not white. I just wish my skin was a little darker, that's all. But it is what it is, and I'm dealing, just like every girl is dealin' with what bugs them. The truth is that on most days, I like a lot about myself."

"And you're beautiful," one of the girls said.

She smiled and sat down. And when she did, I tapped her on the shoulder and nodded my head to let her know I approved whole-heartedly.

"That's right," Mrs. Knight said. "Holly is beautiful."

Her long gorgeous hair went down further than her sister's did. I always thought most black girls with long hair wore a weave, but that wasn't the case. I thanked the Lord for allowing me to be friends with the Nelson sisters.

> "Self-esteem isn't about how someone else thinks you look. It's about how you think you look and feel."

"Miss Thomas, your turn," Mrs. Knight said, putting me on the spot.

The impulse I had to slide down in my seat, like I had done in math class when called upon, was strong. I'd been waiting in this seat for a long time, and now that it was my time, I didn't want to get up.

"You can get up now, dear," she said, embarrassing me in front of everyone. "Self-esteem is the topic. Do you have any personal issues with how you look?"

"How could she?" a girl in the back called out.

"Yeah, she's beautiful," said another.

I stood, feeling even more uncomfortable. "I guess that's it. I am a little shy. I get nice compliments about my looks a lot of times. Self-esteem isn't about how someone else thinks you look. It's about how you think you look and feel. I thought my mom was crazy by wanting me to get involved in this pageant because as I look as around, you are all so much prettier and more poised than I am."

"Oh, come on, girl. We all think you're gonna win," someone said, breaking my concentration.

"I don't know who said that, but I don't feel that way. It's not just one thing that I feel uncomfortable about. I think it's mostly everything. Some days I feel like I can't get up and talk in front of a group or go to a new school and hold my head high. I really didn't wanna be in this pageant at all, not because being Miss Teen Nashville wouldn't be a great honor and all, but because of my insecurities. But I'm here. It's not about the crown anymore because we're all winners if we think that we are beautiful and unique. I can see the crowns on each of our heads. We all have to feel like we deserve to wear that tiara, not to boast about our outer beauty, but to emulate what true beauty really is. I don't know…" I sat down.

"Oh, no. Your response was amazing, Miss Thomas. You said everything I was going to say to close today's session, but you said it better than I ever have," Mrs. Knight said. "Crowns are made with diamonds, and the most expensive diamond still has a flaw. However, that doesn't mean it's worth any

less. So, ladies, get yourselves together and know that you all have it goin' on! You're ladies with poise, charm, wisdom, pizzazz, spunk, charisma, athletic ability, and most importantly, intelligence. Either you want to be here or get out!" she shouted. After she smiled, she snapped her fingers.

I stood up straight and grinned. I felt good. I was totally surprised by confidence.

Conquer Point

Calm down. What good can come from you going off on people? Even though people may deserve to be checked, there is a way to deal with them so they'll listen. Cut people the break that God cuts to you daily and you will live a much happier, stress-free life.

Prayer

All right now, Lord, I need help to step up for myself and to see my beauty. Why haven't I noticed how much other people struggle with the same things I do? Let me use this lesson to be more tolerant and kind toward others...even those I am jealous of or frustrated with. Give me Your tolerance. Show me how to communicate the right way. I'm breaking here. Please hold me together.
Amen.

u Journal

CHAPTER 8:

august

Ended *the* Misery

Sometimes life doesn't seem worth it. I know. I get in major funks and try so hard to claw my way out. I feel so down that I need an escape. If you feel like you don't want to be here and no one cares, you're wrong.

I care, and I really need us both to hang in there.

[CHAPTER 8]
Ended the Misery

Scrapbooking had always been one of my favorite things to do. I used to do lots of pages every weekend, but these days, with school focus, friendship realities, and boy distractions, I found it difficult to barely finish my monthly page. I was committed to that, at least. So when I finally did have a moment, I lay across my mom and dad's king-size canopy bed and began to enjoy my hobby. But I couldn't get too into it because my mom entered the room on the cordless phone sounding all upset.

Without meaning to listen, I heard something I did not want to hear.

"A car accident! Is Rose okay? What about Belle?" Mom was visibly upset as she headed back out to the hallway and out of earshot. I got up and followed her until she hung up the phone. She was starting to cry.

"Mom, you're scaring me. What's going on?"

> **We've got to go. Your Aunt Rose has been in an accident.**

She leaned in, kissed my forehead, and hugged me.

"Mom?" I said, with my voice muffled against her shoulder.

"We've got to go. Your Aunt Rose has been in an accident."

"Is she okay? I heard you mention Belle... was she hurt?"

"Belle is fine. But we aren't sure how your aunt is. All I know is that we need to get to Atlanta now. Go pack."

I looked up at her. I could tell by her face that she was thinking the same thing I was... that this was a lot like last year when we got the call about my grandpa's heart attack.

I scurried to my room and gathered up my things quickly while Mom told Dad, Blake, and Joy. Just like when we were heading out for the tour, we worked together and treated each other with grace. Dad used some connections he had with a travel agent and we all got on a plane for Atlanta in record time.

We took a cab to the hospital from the Atlanta airport. Mom was wringing her hands and making cell calls to other members of the family. Nobody was sure how Rose was doing or what had happened exactly. A nurse called up to the fifth floor and told us we could go on up. When the elevator doors opened to the sterile environment, we all shuddered a little. Then my little cousin Belle came running up. She reminded me of a mini version of Joy with her dark hair and sparkling eyes.

"It's going to be okay, sweetie," I reassured her and hugged her tight.

"They're saying that I might have to go away."

I had no idea what she was talking about, but I had to say something that would make her calm down. "You're not going anywhere. Everything is going to be okay."

"Are you sure, Faith?"

"Of course! I'm your big cousin. I'm going to take care of you."

She hugged my neck tightly and I prayed silently, *Lord, please make the words I told my cousin come true. Help us through this situation. Whatever she's talking about, let her be wrong. Let no one take her away from her mother.* Before I could finish praying, I heard my mom over in the corner arguing with some woman I'd never seen.

"I understand you're just doing your job, but you are not taking my niece into custody. If I have to go to a judge right now and get custody of this child, I will. She could also stay with her grandparents. They live here in town if it is a problem of taking her out of state."

The woman responded, "Because your father is still recovering from his heart attack, we don't think your parents are the best option. They have to worry about all of the doctor's appointments and physical therapy sessions. It isn't the right timing for them. If you want to step forward, then that's a possibility I hope we can make possible."

"*Hope* can make possible? I don't want to talk like that. We need to figure this out right now. I mean, someone needs to explain to me why my sister can't have her child."

All of a sudden, my grandmother yanked my mom's arm and pulled her to the side into another corner and started talking. They got a bit loud.

"Why are they yelling?" my little cousin asked with a trembling lip. I had just calmed her down.

"They aren't yelling, honey. They are just talking loud. Too loud," I said the last part loudly myself so that Mom would catch a clue and calm down.

Two days later, my family and I were on a plane back to Nashville, except we were not alone. A judge had granted temporary guardianship to my parents. I looked over at Belle and smiled to keep reassuring her. The truth was that my aunt was not doing well. It was possible that Belle could legally become my sister.

My mom held her all the way home and told her that everything was going to be okay. However, by the looks on everyone's faces, none of us believed it.

Why did school have to start so soon? Although it was exciting that I was going into the tenth grade, it was going to end my summer fun. No more beaches, swimming pools, or nights staying up late reading, scrapbooking, emailing, or listening to my latest music downloads.

When the first day of school rolled around, our family had been caring for Belle for a couple weeks. My aunt was doing better now that she was in a rehabilitation center, but because her progress was slow, she agreed that Belle was better off with us. The older cousins were able to be on their own with our grandparents checking in on them. My parents also were making sure to call them frequently to be sure they felt supported.

It was surprising how quickly we had settled into a new routine to include our latest addition. Belle's spirit was loving and joyous, and she added a lot of activity to our house. Sometimes it was too much. It reminded me of

---

Value Verse

"Being confident of this, that he who began a good work in you will carry it on to completion until the day of Christ Jesus."

[Philippians 1:6]

when Blake was younger and so full of questions and comments.

Dad was taking me to school. Usually both of my parents took me on the first day, but Mom had a lot to do between watching Belle and preparing for a big photo shoot for one of her contracted models. And I sort of wondered if Dad was taking me so that he could play "protective papa." We hadn't spoken a lot more about the incident with Drew, but once in a while I would see Dad looking at me with a sad face, and he would be lost in thought.

When we pulled up to the school I opened the car door and turned to my dad to say goodbye. He blew me a kiss and told me to have a great first day. "Hey, what are you looking forward to most?" he asked when I had stepped partway out the door.

"Just seeing everyone. And facing classes with more confidence."

I couldn't believe that in my mind I was also thinking, "And I'll see Niles every day." Had I not totally blown the guy off during the summer? I needed to stick to my decision no matter how strong other feelings were.

Dad winked at me. "Knock 'em dead. Love you."

"Love you," I said waving as he pulled away from the curb.

> **"Hey, girl! Are you searching for the guy you don't like?"**

I couldn't believe how I still felt tied to Niles. I knew I felt something, and it was very clear to me that my feelings had not changed even after my "no thanks" conversation with him because I had barely walked onto the school grounds when I caught myself searching for him in the hallway. I didn't see him, but I did see Kendal, and she was heading right for me.

"Hey, girl! Are you searching for the guy you don't like?" she said sarcastically.

"How'd you know?" I laughed with sarcasm, trying to pretend that she was totally wrong.

"'Cause I know you're not looking that hard for me. Or Hope. Or your sister. You can only be scouting like that for a guy."

I elbowed her and tried to ignore her comment. "What classes you got? Do we have something together?"

"Nope. We're on different block schedules."

"Not even math again? This time we'll have to study harder," I said as I tried to look at her schedule in her hand. But as I leaned over, she pulled away from me.

I asked, "What's going on? Why don't you want me to see your schedule?"

I snatched the paper out of her hand and saw what she was hiding. She was repeating algebra.

"What's this?" I asked as I pointed to the dreaded word.

"The teacher found out that I was cheating, okay?"

"How?"

SELF-ESTEEM GROWS

But I Can't…

If God calls you to something, He'll also give you what is needed to carry out the task (2 Corinthians 9:8). When you say that you can't do something God called you to do, you are not operating out of faith. You are saying much more than "I can't." You are saying "God can't." You are saying that the God of the universe, who raises the sun every morning and who made the trees and the ocean and who created us, can't take care of your problems. Don't doubt yourself or what you can do because if you put your toe in the water, God will come across oceans to help you accomplish His purposes. Don't be ashamed of your weaknesses because God does His best work with those that seem the least likely to carry out the task. "'My grace is sufficient for you, for my power is made perfect in weakness.' Therefore I will boast all the more gladly about my weaknesses, so that Christ's power may rest on me" (2 Corinthians 12:9).

[blog]

>>

When people talk about me, it doesn't bother me at all. After all, they talked about Christ and He withstood the blasphemy. He can help me take any scornful blow as well.

<<

Randy | Los Angeles, CA | 13 years old | 9th Grade

"I had the wrong test. She changed it after ten years of having the same one because she heard students were cheating. Anyway, she failed me. I have to take it over. So go ahead and brag or gloat or rag on me. You were right. Cheatin' didn't pay off."

I didn't want to be right. I didn't want my friend to have to take the subject over. She could see in my face that I sincerely hated that. We just hugged, truly understanding each other.

"Hey, girls!" Hope came up to us and bumped the back of our legs, bending both our knees.

"Hope! You've been in hiding all summer. I missed you," I said.

"I decided to spend more time with my family."

"Good for you."

She smiled but shrugged. "It was work, girl, but I do think it was worth it."

Nellie walked by and waved to me but not to the others. I could tell she wanted to talk, but why was she being so distant with them? She wanted my friendship to be exclusive, and I wasn't going to give in to her pouting. But Nellie wasn't the rudest girl I knew. My eyes widened when I saw Leigh, the girl from my private school who had caused me so much drama. She walked up to me like we were best friends.

"Faith Thomas! It's me! I've put aside the prep school uniform and come to join you in the public school world. Give me a hug, girl!"

Hope and Kendal could tell this girl was not my friend.

"You must introduce!" Leigh said, clapping her hands together.

"Umm... I've got to get to class," Kendal said.

"Yeah, me too. See you later," Hope said as she and Kendal dashed off.

Nellie, who had circled back around to where I was standing, leaned in past my shoulder and said, "Well, I'm her best friend, Nellie. And you are?"

"I was her best friend at the private school."

I almost choked when I heard Leigh say that.

"Every party I gave, she was at the top of my invite list. I'll be giving a few parties here. Make sure you come," she said snobbishly.

Nellie just looked at me. I knew she was thinking back to the party I chose to go to instead of spending the night over at her house over a year ago. I remember asking if I could bring Nellie, and Leigh refused because she didn't want the competition of another cute

> " Of all the **guys** **Leigh** could go after, **why** did she have to pick **him?** "

girl. I should have known she was no good at that moment, but it still took me a while to catch on. But this was a new year, and I was much, much wiser.

"What are you doing here, Leigh?"

"Dollars got too tight for my parents, so if you're wondering why I'm here, it's not because I think this is better. I figured if Jack Thomas's daughter could come, this is the public school I needed to attend. Some black girl whose dad is a big gospel singer goes here too."

"His daughters are Hope and Holly, okay, Leigh? I don't recognize my friends by color, and you and I weren't good friends in middle school. Let's not pretend."

"Whatever. Who wants girlfriends anyway? See that cute guy over there? He'll be wanting to go out with me before the end of the day. You're still stuck in middle school, Faith. I can totally tell."

Nellie and I turned around to see who she was looking at. It was Niles. Nellie and I were both shocked. Of all the guys that Leigh could go after, why did she have to pick him? I almost groaned out loud. There was no way I'd be okay with her conquering my man at heart. Leigh turned and walked over to him and began talking. She was twirling her hair and acting all shy and flirty. I couldn't believe it. The next thing I know, he was walking her to class. I was sick and angry.

"Told you my brother was a dog, but you didn't believe me. I'm going to have to tell him about that girl. No way I'd want her as a dating sister-in-law."

I was caring less and less what Nellie thought, but how dare Niles walk with another girl! He probably knew I was standing close by. Whatever I was feeling I had to get it in check. Niles owed me nothing, and even though I hated to admit it, Leigh was cute. I could definitely see him falling for her, and I knew it would tear me up. What was I going to do?

Maybe now was the time to tell him that I did like him, that I did want to get to know him. Would he even listen after I turned him down so coldly over the summer? What was a girl to do?

I didn't have much time over the next few weeks to focus on boy trouble. That was a good thing because I didn't need to be stressed-out. Tenth grade started out strong: quizzes, research projects, cheerleading practices in school, and cheerleading practices at the gym. I had thought about quitting United Storm and just concentrating on one team, but my coach said he needed me. I guess hearing that I was needed made all the difference. I agreed to be on both the school and the private teams.

My emotions were all jumbled about Nellie. We hadn't spoken much, which I figured was exactly how I should want it. However, one evening she was on my heart. I couldn't shake these feelings, and finally I gave in to what the Holy Spirit was working in me. Being a Christian and believing in God is one thing, but exercising that power was something completely different. This desire to connect with Nellie came from God. And if I had been learning anything this past year, it was that these nudges of the Spirit were not to be ignored. I needed to pray about it. God was leading me to do or say something to encourage my friend.

So I picked up the phone and called Nellie on her cell phone. When she answered, she didn't sound right at all. The harshness in her voice was eerie. She could barely keep her breath, and I couldn't make sense of anything she was saying.

"Calm down. Nellie, I can't hear you."

"I'm over at your house. I'm ready to jump in the pond. I want to die."

I hoped she hadn't said what I thought I heard. I kept my phone in my hand and ran downstairs and out the back door as fast as I could. The night was dark, but a lamppost and a string of white lights gave enough light for me to see that there was someone out by our pond.

"Nellie!" I yelled as loudly as I could.

The figure turned, and I hung up the phone and ran toward her. I was breathless when I reached her, so I just hugged her tight for what seemed like several minutes. Without realizing it, I was saying her name over and over and patting her head.

"What happened?" I said after we finally stepped back from one another. I saw tears streaming down her face, and she had a very distant, empty look in her eyes.

Softly she said, "He dumped me. You told me not to get with him. You told me to hold on to my innocence and my sense of value, but I refused to listen." She looked at me after she made this confession. She had not ever told me for sure if she had slept with Ethan. I nodded for her to go on. "I thought he loved me, but he dumped me, Faith. I don't even want to live anymore. I feel worthless."

I couldn't believe what she was saying. I felt my heart stop. Such mixed emotions were rushing through me. My best friend had been used. Now I understood why God gave us guidelines as Christians, as children of God. If we keep ourselves away from sinful behaviors, we wouldn't have to feel such pain, anguish, misery, and rejection. Things didn't work out for Nellie because she had given a part of herself away to a guy who did not understand the importance of who she was. She was hurting because she had given away a part of herself as a way to gain value, and here she was feeling worthless and as though she didn't have a reason to live. I looked at the water rippling in our pond and then at my friend's tear-stained face. I was thankful that God told me to connect with her at that very moment. I needed to tell her that she was special and worthy of life. God created her and she knew this…yet somewhere along the way she had forgotten how very valued that made her.

> "I **thought** he loved me, but he **dumped me**, Faith. I don't even want to **live** anymore. I **feel** worthless."

Nellie walked closer to the pond. *Lord, You've got to help me connect with her.* All of a sudden, I ran up to her, grabbed her hand, and squeezed it tight, and my mouth began to move and words came out.

"Listen. You were the one who told me about God. Yeah, you made a mistake. Yeah, you lost a precious part of you. But that doesn't mean you can't be pure again. You know the One who can restore you and make you whole."

"But I don't deserve God's love. I knew what I shouldn't do. How could God forgive me? I tried to justify it by saying God gave me the feelings for Ethan, but all along I knew I just

AUGUST

SOMETHING TO DO
Visit a homeless shelter and work in a soup kitchen.

THINK ABOUT IT
Have you showed the people you love how much you care about them?

HISTORY LESSON
Anne Frank was a Jewish girl who hid from the Nazis with her family and a few others in a secret annex behind her father's office. They lived there for two years, and Anne journaled during that time. Her last entry was in August 1944. "The Diary of Anne Frank" is one of the most powerful books ever printed. If you haven't read it yet... read it!

HOLIDAYS/DATES IN HISTORY
August 1, 1969 → Birth of the Internet's structure
August 10, 1846 → The Smithsonian Institute created
August 21, 1958 → Hawaii becomes 50th state

HAPPY BIRTHDAY TO YOU
Marques Houston → August 4
Ben Affleck → August 15
Jeff Stinco → August 22
Cameron Diaz → August 30

Faith's Timeline
Aug. 4th → Belle comes to live with us
19th → First day of school
24th → Nellie is still here! Thank the Lord.
Mondays, Wednesdays, Thursdays, Saturdays: cheer practice

[Beauty is] a kind of radiance. People who possess a true inner beauty— their eyes are a little brighter, their skin a little more dewy. They vibrate at a different frequency.

CAMERON DIAZ

wanted Ethan to like me, to say I was pretty and worth loving."

"Nellie, let God restore you. Trust Him to fix this."

The wind started blowing hard. It felt like a sign. It felt like God was telling her that He could blow away the anguish.

"Thank you, Faith," she said as she and I gripped hands. "Thank you for giving me grace and for reminding me of God's grace. I made a mistake, but I want to keep living."

Hearing those words come from my friend made me weak in the knees. I was so very grateful to God. What if I hadn't felt His leading? What if I had ignored it? Life as a teen was tough. We weren't going to get it right all the time. But we knew God, and He would always help us through. I knew Nellie would not only have to receive God's grace, but she would have to regain her sense of wholeness and value. It would be a long road for her, but now I was able to walk beside her.

Nellie and I linked arms and headed back to my house, relieved and thankful that God had ended the misery.

Conquer Point

No one can make you want to move past your burdens but you. Know that things will be okay because God cares enough about you to fix it. Pity parties make things worse, but praising the Lord in the midst of your pain will help heal your broken heart.

Prayer

Father, I honestly don't want to go on. I hate my life and I want the pain to stop. However, I know Your will for me is to trust You and live through this. So please help me. I want to get stronger from my anguish and grow to be a better Christian. In Jesus' name, amen.

u Journal

CHAPTER 9:

september

Renewed My Beliefs

Okay, so today is a better day for me. I hope it is for you as well. Things aren't perfect, but I have perspective. I am recommitting my life to Christ. I want to be happy whether things go my way or not. It's not about what I don't have, but it's about what I do have. My God—my heavenly Father—loves me. And He loves you too.

What good news!

[CHAPTER 9]

Renewed *My* Beliefs

It was time for me to go to bed. I needed all the sleep I could get these days. School was busy and challenging. But the grumbling in my stomach made me detour from the hall toward my bedroom to the kitchen. On my way, I considered whether I was in a salty or sweet food mood.

Mom had put Belle to bed an hour before, but on my way past her door I heard her crying. The door was ajar, so I pushed it open a bit further and saw Belle curled up in her bed, weeping. Seeing her so sad broke my heart, but I figured she'd stop crying. I mean, she was in a new place, after all. I was tempted to keep walking. Was I really up for this tonight? But my feet ignored my growling stomach and they stood, frozen in front of the doorway.

"Knock, knock," I said.

I was afraid I wouldn't know how to comfort Belle. I was in high school and she was in kindergarten. What could I say to make her feel better? When she didn't even acknowledge that I was standing in the room, I realized how upset she really was. Somehow, the Lord would have to help me help her. I walked in and sat on her bed.

"It's okay, Belle," I whispered, hoping she'd turn around and smile, but of course she didn't. She just cried harder.

"I want my mommy. I don't want to be here anymore."

What could I say to that? I didn't want to lie, and I didn't know if she'd see her mom soon. I didn't know if she'd be living with us forever. Even though I didn't remember what it was like to be five, I knew that if I were in her shoes, I certainly wouldn't want anyone filling my head up with false hope. I pulled her into my arms and cradled her. I wiped away the tears from her warm cheeks. I rubbed her soft, brown hair and spoke words from the center of my heart.

> "I **realized** what I could do was to **tell her** about the One who **loved** her more than anybody."

"I know it has gotta be a little sad being in a new place, and I'm sure you miss your mom and your older brothers a lot. You probably don't think it's ever going to feel better."

"It won't."

"I know how you feel. I used to think life couldn't get better."

"You did?" She took a deep sniffle.

I realized what I could do was to tell her about the One who loved her more than anybody. I could tell her about the One who would be there for her always, the One who helped turn my life around.

"I believe in Jesus. And Jesus is the One who is with us when we are sad, alone, or hurting, Belle."

"I know Jesus," she said, surprising me.

"And what do you know about Him?"

100 | Faith Thomas Series Vol. 2

"I believe He is God's Son, that He is up in heaven, and that He loves me."

"You know so much, Belle! And if we believe those things about Him, then we can also trust that He's got us in His hand. Do you trust that?"

"Yep. He's got the whole world in His hand."

"He does, Belle," I said laughing at her use of a song title. The Lord did have the whole world in His hand, and that meant that He had Belle's mom and her future in a tight grasp. "You're safe," I said. "The Lord loves your mom. He's going to take care of her while you are apart, and you don't have to be scared because so many of us are here for you. But if you want someone to be with you all the time, then just remember that Jesus is with you. You'll never be left alone. I don't know how long you're going to be with us, but we're going to make it a good time. I know your mom would want you to be happy, and who couldn't be happy knowing that God is always looking out for them, right?"

"Right."

She hugged me tightly, and I noticed that her tears had already dried. As I encouraged her, I was encouraging myself too. Things were going very well because I had changed my mind-set. I started to think more positively and be more excited about life instead of stressing the small stuff. I understood that God had it all. And if He had it all, then I didn't have to worry.

BEHIND THE SCENES ON BELLE

FULL NAME: Belle Macy Blake
BIRTH DATE: September 21
FAMILY MAKEUP: Mom, older brothers, aunt, uncle, and cousins
FAVORITE COLOR: Purple
FAVORITE FOOD: Ice cream
HOBBIES: Ballet and tap
GOALS: Wants to go home to her mom and not be afraid of the dark.
STRENGTHS: Makes everyone smile
WEAKNESS: Sheds crocodile tears at the drop of a hat
ONE POSITIVE ABOUT THIS CHARACTER: Trusting
WORD OF INFLUENCE: Smile
FAVORITE PHRASE: I love you.

The weekend was here, and it was a beautiful day. My Saturday was full. I went to the gym for cheerleading practice, to the civic center for pageant practice, to the studio with my dad to record a song, and then back home to hang out with some girlfriends to end the day. Kendal, Hope, and Nellie would arrive soon. I rushed through the house gathering extra pillows so we could lounge around and picked out a few magazines I thought would be fun to go through.

> "We both know **how hard** it can be to find a **true friend**. Give them a **chance**, Nellie."

When the three were all standing in the living room, it was sort of awkward. I mean, Kendal and Hope already hung out together, but Nellie was standoffish. I didn't understand what her problem was, and it was clear that my other two friends didn't, either. I almost wished she hadn't come, but then I thought about how depressed she had been. This seemed like just the way to draw her out of a place of anger and negativity. But I had some serious doubts when, after an hour, Nellie still had not warmed up to anyone. When she headed to the bathroom, the rest of us looked at one another. I knew I was going to get an earful.

Hope looked at me and raised her eyebrows. "What's going on with her? I mean, is it me? Has she never hung out with a black girl before?"

"No, it's not like that."

"Maybe she doesn't like that I'm not...you know, one of you," Kendal said from behind me.

"One of who?"

"A Christian. I'm assuming she is, right?"

"No. I mean, yes, she is a Christian, but she's not judgmental about you not being one. Trust me. She's learning that we all fall. She's had it tough lately. I thought this could be good for her, but maybe she isn't ready for a girls' day."

"Uh, yeah. I would say she's not ready. Maybe she should've stayed home," Hope said loud enough for Nellie to hear when she came back to the room.

Nellie didn't respond to Hope, but she turned to me and said, "If you want to hang with me, Faith, like you said we would, then I'll be in the backyard hammock waiting. For a while, anyway."

Nellie stormed out the French doors and stomped over to the hammock. I let out a big sigh and told Kendal and Hope to give me a minute with Nellie before they followed me out there.

"Don't you worry about that. We'll give you and the Ice Queen all the space you need. Hope and I will hang near the snacks."

Hope nodded in complete agreement. "Yes... go tell the Ice Queen to chill for us."

They laughed and I worked up the courage to face Nellie and her stormy mood. I walked outside. The warmth of the fall air soothed me a bit and I felt a little less anxious. However, when I saw Nellie's stern look as I approached her, I could feel my mood turning quickly.

"What's up with you?" I blurted out.

Value Verse

"We are God's workmanship, created in Christ Jesus to do good works, which God prepared in advance for us to do."

[Ephesians 2:10]

Nellie didn't waste any time giving me a piece of her mind. "Why couldn't I just come? Why did you have to invite them too? You don't like being my best friend anymore because of what I did, is that it? Are you afraid to be alone with me because of how messed up I was the other night by the pond?"

My heart softened a little toward Nellie. I needed to remember how very raw she was and how vulnerable. "That's not it, Nellie. I totally wanted to spend this time with you. It's just that I spend time with those two as well, and I wanted them to get to know you...my best friend."

Nellie's scowl softened for a second at the term "best friend." She looked up at me as though asking if I was sure.

"Yes. I said you are my best friend, but that doesn't mean you are my only friend. I thought we could all get along and really connect. Maybe it's too soon for you and you'd rather be alone?"

"There were some things I wanted to talk to you—and only you—about, but I suppose I also need these kinds of days too. I could use some fun. I'm just so messed up now, Faith."

"I understand. And I think you're absolutely right...you need fun. We don't always have to do things together as a foursome, but couldn't we try this group and see if it works? We both know how hard it can be to find a true friend. Give them a chance, Nellie."

As if on cue, Hope and Kendal came outside. They eyed me to be sure the coast was clear. I nodded to them and waved them over to the hammock.

Hope stepped up closest to Nellie and said, "Hey, I'm sorry that I was ragging on you. That was unfair of me and not a very godly attitude. Faith thinks you're the greatest, and I know we'll all connect if we give it time, right, Kendal?" Hope jabbed Kendal in the ribs and Kendal gave her a sideways "do I have to?" glare.

"Right. If we give each other a chance," Kendal said half convincingly.

Just then Joy came out on the deck. "I want to try out my new camera. Everybody get on the hammock. This will be the perfect group shot." My sister was oblivious to the tensions we had all just been feeling. She motioned for Kendal to sit down next to me and for Hope to sit down next to Nellie. We all looked at one another and laughed.

We posed for the camera over and over again, getting sillier and sillier. Joy called out orders for how to smile, how to pose, how to position our heads.

"Geez, Joy," I said. "What are you...a director now?"

"Mom said I'd do better with modeling if I understood camera angles and what makes a good photo."

It felt so good to be laughing and enjoying a group of friends. Everyone must have felt the same way because after Joy headed inside, Nellie turned to me and whispered, "Sorry about my mood swing. Having fun and being with new people is what I needed. I like them. I shouldn't get so jealous."

We kept whispering.

"You don't have to worry about me not

[blog]

>>

I find that when I tell my self good things, good things happen. It's like I'm letting the Holy Sprit loose... and it's all good.

<<

Kelly | Tupelo, MS | 13 years old | 8th Grade

---

making time for us. You're my best friend for a reason. You get me, and even though I didn't agree with your choices recently, it was because I cared about you. We're not supposed to be the same, but we should be able to help each other grow, especially in our faith, but also in other friendships."

"Yeah," she said as she looked at me sincerely. "I've got to let you be friends with whoever."

"Y'all got this thing worked out now?" Hope said and then smiled. "Because I'm gettin' hungry."

"Last one to the kitchen—" I said.

"Please don't say 'is a rotten egg,'" Kendal interrupted.

We all looked at each other and took off running. We ran on the deck. We ran in the yard. We were being silly and rowdy and carefree and honest. I was enjoying my friends, and I thanked God I could be real with them. This was a big change from where my life was a year and a half ago. I had no friends then, but now I had three great ones. Seeing how God was showing up and revealing Himself in my life made me want to keep trusting Him.

I couldn't believe the pageant was really happening. My family and friends were in the audience. Throughout the first part of the program I had allowed myself to look over at them every now and then. I realized, though, that I needed to stay focused or it was easy to become nervous. When I took each step walking in godly confidence and offering my fears up to the Lord, I was able to remain calm and in the moment. With God guiding me, it didn't matter what the end result would be; it only mattered that I was trusting Him.

The ten finalists for the Miss Teen Nashville title were about to be announced. All of the competitors were filing out to their positions on stage. Just before I walked through the curtains and out to the main area, Holly tapped me on the shoulder and winked at me.

"I think both of us have a chance to win this thing. It's been fun going through it with you. You're real cool, Faith. I see why my sister likes you so much."

I just smiled. It's always nice to be told something positive. I was finally learning to take in some of the practices I'd learned during the pageant training. For example,

> " With God **guiding me**, it didn't matter what the **end result** would be. It only mattered that I was **trusting** Him. "

when you are given a compliment, just say thank you. You don't have to give one back because you feel obligated. And you don't have to dismiss it as if you don't deserve it, which is what I always used to do. Just accept it and be appreciative of it.

When they began to call names, I found myself relieved and excited to hear my own among the ten who would remain for the next portion of the pageant. It was more than I could imagine, and thankfully Holly was also standing there. Jillian was too. I knew that if I didn't go any further, I would be completely proud of myself. I was proud to be in this pageant. I loved my city. I loved the "me" God created. Walking out on stage in the evening gown, I held my head high. I imagined that the spotlights were stars guiding me on my way.

During the swimsuit competition, I was a little uncomfortable. I wasn't exactly thrilled to stand in front of a full crowd wearing just a one-piece and my sash. I got a lot of applause when my name was again called, this time for the final five. I wondered what in the world the Lord was doing.

Next it was time for the talent competition. Last month I was sort of resisting the idea of singing for my talent section. I mean, who wants to be compared to their famous father all the time? He was such a great singer, and I was still trying to be brave enough to get through a full song. But after a lot of prayer and practicing, I decided to commit to singing.

I sat on a stool with one light shining down on me. I wanted the performance to be simple because I wanted my message to stand out. I sang a song I composed called "God Can Work It Out." The words meant a lot to me and helped me realize that I wasn't in this competition alone. As I told my cousin Belle, God is with us always. His Spirit was giving me the confidence to not stress. When I sang the last line: "Now that I have faith and believe that, I'm

worry free," folks stood to their feet and clapped for me. The applause really caught me off guard. I felt like I was on stage with my father. I hadn't expected such a response, so I responded a bit awkwardly with a half bow and something like a curtsey and then rushed to the back. Holly passed me and gave me a quick pat on the back. "Good job!" she said, beaming. She was on her way to perform.

To an audience in awe, Holly played the saxophone and did a beautiful job. Nobody expected the pretty athlete to have such musical talents. Next, Jillian twirled a flaming baton, and she did well too. I never felt that I wanted either of them to do badly, even though crazy Jillian was a bit mean at times, I kept giving her the benefit of the doubt because I knew she wanted the title more than anyone.

Soon it was time for questions and I was up. The host picked a question from a fishbowl and read it out loud to me. "If you were Miss Teen Nashville, what would you say to other young girls who didn't feel pretty?"

He handed me the mic and I gripped it tightly. I held my head up high and said, "If I were Miss Teen Nashville, it would be my honor to tell all young women that they are unique and special. I would encourage them to believe in themselves and follow their dreams, and if they do these things, they will feel free, which to me is the feeling of beauty. Yes, every girl who entered this pageant is beautiful, but every girl living in Nashville is also beautiful."

I received cheers. It was sort of fun just answering truthfully. When it was time for the final scores to be read, I noticed I was still standing in place after he called the fourth place winner and the third place winner. I looked around, and Holly, Jillian, and I were the last three standing. We held hands and braced ourselves. Then the emcee called on Holly as the second runner-up. Jillian and I let go of Holly's hand, and I gave Holly a huge hug. She whispered in my ear, "Go, girl!"

Jillian grabbed my hand again and squeezed it. We both were excited. I couldn't believe that the Lord had brought me this far. With my heart beating fast, I squeezed Jillian's hand back. I wished her luck and meant it. This was all about God's will for my life and not my desires. He had been showing me the entire way that I just needed to trust His power in me and to be faithful to the abilities and hope He planted in my heart and soul.

All things were working out for good. I understood that God allowing me to get this far was a great gift. As one of the last two contestants, it didn't matter to me what the outcome would be in the next few seconds. For me, I had already won. I was stronger, more aware of God's love, and willing to shine—I had renewed my beliefs.

Conquer Point

Think positive. Expect greatness. Look for the best in every situation. Help others. Be genuine. Love hard. Learn from your mistakes. Enjoy being a teen. You don't have to be down on yourself. You do have it going on. Regain and maintain your confidence.

Prayer

Dear Lord, wow I feel great today. Nothing major is happening. I just feel Your presence and it's wonderful. Help me continue to be this way. I know it pleases You to see me walk in faith. Thanks for taking care of me.

In Jesus' name, amen.

SEPTEMBER

Think About It

Think about how the world has changed since the September 11 attacks on the World Trade Center in 2001. How do you hope the world will be in five more years? Ten? Fifty? How do you plan to make it a better world?

Holidays

Labor Day → September 3
Autumn begins → September 22

Happy Birthday to You

Michelle Williams → September 9
Prince Harry → September 15
Avril Lavigne → September 27
Hilary Duff → September 28

Something to Do

Hispanic Heritage Month starts on the fifteenth, wear something with a Hispanic influence to show support.

History Lesson

On September 11, 2001, two planes crashed into the twin towers of the World Trade Center in New York City, killing the pilots, the passengers, people in the tower buildings, and many police and firefighters who went in to save them. Two other planes were hijacked that day, and one crashed into the Pentagon and the other went down in a field in Pennsylvania because it is believed that the passengers on that flight fought the terrorists while in flight.

Faith's Timeline

Sept. 15th → Slumber party planned for my girls
21st → Belle's birthday
Mondays, Wednesdays, Thursdays, Saturdays: cheer practice

Why should I care what other people think of me?

I am who I am. And who I wanna be.
AVRIL LAVIGNE

CHAPTER 10:

october

Betrayed but Positive

It's easy to say we'll get them next time, but it's harder to actually feel content when things don't work out as you planned. However, I think I'm really growing here. I now can be happy for others when things in their lives work out. I no longer want to sweat the small stuff, and I feel so much happier on the inside. Yep, I'm feeling better.

I hope you're positive too.

[CHAPTER 10]

Betrayed *but* Positive

Standing in the colorful gown my mom picked out for me was a great moment. The dress was beautiful, with fabric of cyan, sunny orange, and hot pink cascading down from a blue corset top. I felt like royalty. It was a special moment because this journey through the pageant had been so much more about life's journey than I would have imagined. Before this, my visions of a pageant were of hundreds of girls who looked just like Jillian and who presumed they were superior. Instead I discovered that inside all girls are special and also very similar. I knew this would serve me well throughout my life. My pursuits would never be about being better than others, but would be about being my best self, the best Faith God created.

I glanced at my parents, Blake, and Joy. Their faces were filled with anticipation. The emcee was ready to announce this year's winner. I stood holding Jillian's hand.

"The first runner-up is…Miss Faith Thomas."

Everyone clapped for me as I went up and received my award. Cameras from the audience and the media area flashed, and I walked back and stood by Jillian who had a huge winner's smile on her face. She was containing her emotion until the emcee could officially state the results. "Our new Miss Teen Nashville is Jillian Gray!"

Jillian started screaming in my ear and shaking frantically. It was a bit over the top, but that was okay. The Lord prepared me for my place in this whole thing. I had peace before the results were even announced, and I certainly was going to stand on how I felt. I hugged Jillian and spoke to her sincerely.

"Congratulations!" I said as I jumped up and down with her.

I watched her walk to the center of the stage waving her hands and covering her mouth. Cameras were flashing now more than ever as she was crowned and walked from one end of the stage to the other. I was happy for her. I was glad I felt upbeat about her winning. That's what being a good competitor is all about.

After a standing ovation for all the girls, we did our last round of hugs and then were free to walk out to be with our family and friends.

Mom came running up to me first.

"Mom, I'm sorry. I know you wanted the crown. You're the pageant girl in this family. I just don't think it's meant for me."

She didn't say anything. She had a grin on her face, but I didn't understand why.

"Mom, I'm not doing this again next year," I stated in case she was getting ready to sweet-talk me into another try.

"I'm not trying to make you go through it again, but it wasn't that painful, was it?" She gave me a hug and said in my ear, "Faith, I'm smiling because I'm so proud of you! You did this even though it was not an easy choice. I knew you had it in you all the time, and now I think you believe it too, right?"

Just before the rest of my family reached me, I whispered, "Yes. I believe it."

My dad was scheduled to be promoting his album that day, but he had made time to come. "Oh, honey! The way you sang and

110 | Faith Thomas Series Vol. 2

handled yourself up there in front of everyone was wonderful. The world has not heard the last of you, my dear Faith!"

I half laughed and said, "Dad, I just told Mom that I'm not doing this again."

"Mark my words…they will hear more from Faith Thomas in the future."

> "…this **journey through** the pageant had been **so much** more about **life's** journey than I would have **imagined**."

"I can enter next year," Joy said as she popped in between the two of us.

"And you'd be great," I told my sister. I realized that deep down she wanted the spotlight I had tonight. The pageant had changed me for the better. What was wrong with everyone shining?

Before I left the center, I went up to Jillian and looked her in the face. "You're gonna be great at this."

"I just can't believe how supportive you are," she said to me. "I feel bad because if I had lost, I don't know that I'd even be speaking to you."

"Well, you didn't lose."

"Yeah. But now you're sort of showing me I should have."

"Maybe you will enjoy the experience even more if you believe others want to support you."

Jillian's expression was serious at first and then she smiled broadly. "I learned a lot from you, Faith. Can we hang out sometime?"

"Sure. Take care of the crown."

We hugged. I was truly excited for Jillian, Miss Teen Nashville.

"So why can't we be friends?" Leigh came up to me at school and asked.

When we attended private Christian school, Leigh was the ringleader for all things dramatic and mean. Now she had the audacity to stand in front of me when I was finally enjoying school and a group of real friends and ask why we couldn't be friends.

"I'm not even going to answer that," I finally said.

"Okay, okay. I treated you a little badly, but I think it's more than that. I think you're jealous because I've got your boyfriend. From what I hear, you still don't date. At all."

I don't know what it was with Leigh, but she knew how to get under my skin for real. Maybe she was just bluffing so she could get a rise out of me. She had my number. She was talking about Niles. I'd seen the two of them walking around school together. I tried to act as if it didn't matter, but it ate me up inside. She wasn't a nice girl at all.

"Come on, girl! Let's go to class," Nellie yelled across the hall to me, but before I walked over to her, Leigh opened her big mouth.

"Your best friend is his sister? Before the semester is over, I'll bet she realizes, just like her brother did, that I'm more fun to hang out with than you are."

I wanted to slap her, but instead I prayed, **Lord, forgive me. Help me to remain calm.** I

Value Verse

"To each one of us grace has been given as Christ apportioned it."

[Ephesians 4:7]

Betrayed but Positive | 111

turned and walked over to Nellie, and then we walked toward class.

"What's wrong with you?" Nellie asked.

"I'm okay," I said, raising my hand in the air and pushing all that behind me.

> "…you're **jealous** because I've got your **boyfriend**. From what I hear, **you** still don't date. **At all**."

"You can tell me. She was talking about Niles, huh? You really do like my brother?"

"I can't even believe you're asking me about him again. You don't want to know," I said, frustrated. After all, Nellie was the real reason why I never gave Niles a chance. Yes, I wanted to focus on my relationship with the Lord, but who's to say that being friends with Niles would have been so bad spiritually? Girls can handle guys as friends without falling in sin or giving up everything else that is important to them.

"What? You're gonna blame me?"

I hated that she knew what I was thinking. Agitated, I boldly said, "Yeah, I am!" Then, when I saw Nellie's look of shock and hurt, I explained my emotions. "I'm sorry. I'm mad at Leigh, not you. She just said that you'll end up liking her more than me just like Niles did. And look at me—with this behavior, I'm pushing you toward her."

"She said what?" Nellie asked incredulous. "I would never want to hang out with her. And as far as my brother goes, he thinks she's a complete nut case. Trust me. Now that I've seen some of the dating alternatives around here for Niles, I kinda wish I hadn't discouraged you from getting with him."

"Gee, thanks so much," I said, rolling my eyes.

Nellie sighed and smiled. "In case you didn't notice, that was my attempt at an apology. I blew it, and all because I was jealous."

"You're positive they're not dating?"

"He's right over there. Why don't you go ask him?"

"No. I'll look like an idiot."

"Go…ask…him," she said emphasizing each word and pointing at him. "Go to him before Miss Insane Asylum traps him into another boring conversation about how important her family is and why she's going to public school only to be more in touch with the little people of the world."

I hugged my friend, and then we both walked over to her brother. She knew I needed her support. Even though I had treated Niles coldly when he said he liked me, I had to believe that there could still be a chance.

"Hey!" he said in such a nice way. Nellie smiled at me and walked on to class.

"You put me at ease," I said to him shyly.

"That's a good thing, right?" he asked with a huge smile.

"Yeah. It's a good thing…a very rare thing."

"You headed to class?"

"I am. What about you?"

SELF-ESTEEM GROWS

Sin

Sin is the only thing that stands between you and your accomplishment of the purposes of God. Sin messes with you and turns your head around. It will get you thinking that you need that sin to have life itself! But that is a lie. You don't need sin to get through this life or the next with joy and peace. Recognize sin for what it is! The work of the evil one to keep you away from God's path for your life. Don't embrace sin or defend it in your life. Keeping on a sinful path will never work out for you. It may give you some temporary pleasure, but in the long run it will steal your joy and leave you empty inside. "The wages of sin is death" (Romans 6:23). Always remember that you have the power through Christ to triumph over sin and kick it to the curb like trash. You are never without a choice, no matter how depressed, helpless, or trapped you feel in a situation. God is always a breath away from helping you work it out. Just remember to choose Christ.

[blog]

›› I'm not perfect, and I'm so glad I can confess my sins to God and feel better. ‹‹

Seanaa | Richmond, VA | 14 years old | 9th Grade

"To the cafeteria for my lunch break."

"Which way are you going? I can walk with you."

He was so nice! We started to walk, and with each step I became a bit more courageous. "I want to ask you something I have no right to ask."

"Ask."

"Okay." I hesitated and then continued slowly. "Are you and Leigh seeing each other?"

"No, though she's come on pretty strong."

"Are you seeing anybody?"

"You told me you had one question, and I answered it. Now I think I get a turn before you get another one."

I swallowed. "Okay. Go ahead."

"Would you care if she and I were together?"

I became bashful yet again and turned away. He walked around to position his face close to mine.

"I think your body language has told me the answer I was looking for. I don't think you're quite ready just yet. When you want to talk to me and hang out, you know where I live."

He kissed me on the cheek and walked away. Then Leigh walked over to me and said, "What was my boyfriend doing kissing you?"

Everything she had told me wasn't true, and that in and of itself made me feel good. I looked at her and said, "I don't know why he kissed me, but it sure was nice."

I wasn't trying to hurt her feelings. I barely was aware of her at all. My thoughts were on Niles. I had kept him away before, and it touched my heart that he was letting me back in.

"I cannot believe it has gone this far. We should have taken measures right away. I told you!" Mom was yelling, and I could hear her throughout the house as I got ready for school.

Joy ran up to my room. "Faith! It's Mom and Dad again. This isn't good."

"What's going on?"

"I don't know. But they got a call early this morning, and then there was something in the newspaper that was bad because Mom's been waving the front page around while she was yelling."

I went downstairs. They'd probably tell me to stay out of it, but I was tired of being treated like a little girl.

"Everything's okay, Faith. Head on to school," my dad said, exactly what I thought he would say.

Joy came up behind me, and soon after, Blake showed up with wide eyes and a look of concern.

"Kids, seriously. Go ahead to school. We'll have a family meeting after school. I promise."

I looked at my siblings and they nodded. We agreed to go on to school with the condition that we would discuss the details later.

When I got to school, Hope and Kendal rushed up to me.

"Okay. You need to stay behind us," Hope said.

"We've got your back," Kendal said.

"My back for what?"

I had no idea what they were talking about.

OCTOBER

SOMETHING TO DO
Raise money for a nonprofit. Or donate food to a shelter.

think about it
Try dressing up as something uplifting for Halloween.

history lesson
On October 1, 1957, the motto "In God We Trust" first appeared on United States paper currency when it was added to the one-dollar silver certificate.

HOLIDAYS
Halloween → October 31

HAPPY BIRTHDAY TO YOU

Ashlee Simpson → October 3
Nicky Hilton → October 5
Usher → October 14
Ciara → October 25

Faith's Timeline
Oct. 1st → First runner-up to Miss Teen Nashville
25th → Big news story breaks
Mondays, Wednesdays, Thursdays, Saturdays: cheer practice

> Cry it out. I think crying is definitely something good to do.
> — CIARA

A moment later, Nellie walked up and gave me a sympathetic hug.

"I'm so sorry."

"Okay, you're all officially scaring me."

Before any of them could explain, Leigh came over my way.

"So how does it feel? You think you are so pretty, so special, and now you are knocked off your pedestal. Now everyone knows how messed up your family is."

"Why are you even mentioning my family?"

"Maybe because you are all on the front of the newspaper."

Plain as day, the headline read: "Christian Band Drummer Sues Lead for Illegal Firing and Harassment."

No wonder my mom had been freaking out the last few months. She probably had known this was coming. I could only imagine the gossip that was among those words. Why in the world was this happening to my family?

"Cat got your tongue?" Leigh said with a snide smirk.

Lord, You've gotta help me here. Please take care of whatever trouble is brewing. I'm trying not to lose it here, but, Lord, this is hard.

"Oh! You can't comment? I guess the prideful will fall," Leigh said with amazing coldness.

"Okay, **you** need to leave." Hope stood between Leigh and me.

Kendal took me over to the side when Leigh would not walk away.

"A lot of people are talking about the article. We didn't want you to go into hiding, so we thought we'd all surround you and take care of anyone dumb enough to want to comment."

Nellie came over and entered our conversation. She tried to cheer me up as well.

"This guy, the drummer, he sounds like a total jerk. Nobody believes what he is saying about you or your family. Did you really not know there was legal trouble?"

"My parents were arguing this morning. They said we'd talk about it this evening. I don't know why they let me walk into something like this."

Conquer Point

Now you're getting the point. Life isn't about having all the answers—it's about trusting the One who has all the answers. If there are challenges in your life, look for the lesson to be learned. Stay upbeat and you'll stay happier.

"So it's true?" Hope said as she entered our conversation.

"I don't know what any of this is about. Though if it involves the drummer, it scares me a little. What does the article say?"

My three friends pulled me over to a bench and sat me down. Kendal sat on one side, Nellie was on the other, and Hope sat on the ground in front of me with the paper.

"I'll spare you my bad reading, but basically the drummer is suing your dad and the management company because he says he was illegally fired after your dad found out that you had a crush on him."

"Maybe it would've been better to not know what was in the article," Kendal said.

"No, I needed to know. I can't believe my folks didn't warn us. Poor Joy and Blake." I shook my head with worry.

Hope patted my hand. "Girl, you are getting the worst of it in this article…you and your dad. Your brother and sister will be fine."

"What did happen, Faith? Can you talk about it?" Nellie asked with sympathy in her eyes.

I hadn't told anyone other than family about what the guy had done to me in the bathroom. I had really hoped to move on from it without all of this attention. The nerve of that guy turning it around and acting like **he's** the victim. Encircled by my supportive friends, I relayed the events of that awful evening at the hotel. I cried a little as I shared and then realized it was so much better to get this out. I knew they'd have my back, just like God.

I had to trust Him. Life was crazy, but He prepared me for this. God did have my back. He showed me that time and time again. I had to stay strong because that's what God expected of me. It was weird. I was sort of on a high and a low at the same time. I felt betrayed but positive.

"Disgusting. I never had a crush on him. The guy came after me."

Hope scanned the article for a few minutes and then said, "The drummer says he called you pretty and your dad immediately fired him …which he finds strange because your family displayed you like a prize for a beauty pageant, so obviously they don't mind you being called pretty when it serves their publicity purposes." Hope looked up at me sadly. "Sorry. His quote ends with him saying your dad and your mom will probably turn this mess in to a way to promote your dad's CD and your mom's talent agency."

Prayer

Father, I felt totally betrayed today, but I'm starting to understand that I'm not here to have things perfect for me. I'm here to praise Your name and tell people about how great You are. Thanks for helping me see my purpose. In Jesus' name, amen.

CHAPTER 11:

november

Beamed *with* Pride

It's okay to take a compliment and stand on the mountaintop of your life from time to time. That mountaintop is the time when good things just keep happening. I believe God takes us there to show us that He can do anything but fail. The next time you are feeling great, give God a shout out and take in that precious moment. *You'll need that memory to help get you through a down day.*

[CHAPTER 11]
Beamed with Pride

When Holly stopped me at school, I wasn't sure what was up. With Holly, one could never tell.

"You're strong, Faith Thomas. I like that. All this talk about what that guy did and then the stuff he is saying about your family…you've really held it together. People haven't been able to break you. I admire that."

"I haven't been feeling tough at all."

"I think that's what I learned in that pageant," she said to me. "I mean, I admit. I'm a competitor, and I would've liked to have won, but honestly, I thought you should've got it. You are tough, but you also have a good heart, Faith."

I shook my head. I hadn't been feeling very good about myself lately. I knew that my dad's band was in jeopardy because of what happened between Drew and me that night. And my entire family had been dragged through the mud for a couple weeks in the papers. It was almost like everyone wanted Drew to be right about the situation.

"I'm serious. But, hey, we were the top dogs in the contest. And I did take one important lesson away from the whole pageant thing."

"What's that?"

"Self-esteem lies within. Other people can't shake you, break you, or tear you down. I mean, they can if you let them. But from what I see, you haven't let anybody. I guess that's what I admire. I remember when stuff hit about my dad being this hypocritical Christian. He ruined my seventh-grade year."

I couldn't believe she was being so open with me and telling me that I was doing okay. Maybe that was the Lord's way of showing me, step-by-step and little-by-little, that I could keep on walking with my head up high. I was getting through all this.

"Thank you for the encouragement. I've gotta admit, I've been feeling low."

"What are friends for?"

We both stood still in our tracks. I don't think she realized that she said it, and I couldn't believe that's what I heard her say. Then she let out a sigh.

"So what? We can be friends. Who would've thought it, right?"

I smiled and held out my hand for her to swipe with her fist.

When I got home, I noticed that my dad's car was in the garage. He and I hadn't spent time together lately. He actually hadn't been home. Every time I asked my mom about it, she said he was dealing with his publicist. I knew he was putting out fires. I found my dad in his studio in the basement. He was just staring at the keys. I began singing.

It's okay to be down once in a while.

But even in those times, God wants you to smile.

It may hurt, and it may not feel good.

But in your down time, remember the cross where Jesus stood.

He stood steadfast for you. He bled and died 'cause His love is true.

And even though things right now don't seem fine,

God wants you to rely on Him. God wants you to shine.

My dad stood up from the keyboard and came over to me and held me so tight.

"We have to record that now. I hate all that is going on right now and how you have been hurt by it, but, Faith, God gave you the song to express it all just perfectly."

"Really?" I asked with surprise.

"Before you didn't think you could do it. What changed?"

I pulled away gently, looked into his eyes, and said, "But I can now, Dad. I can sing for God. Those words poured out of me. I'm learning that it is in the lowest times that God wants us to shine with His love and grace."

Dad and I shared something special that evening. When he finished laying the track, I was crying happy tears. I was overjoyed with anticipation of what God was going to do next.

"What a beautiful song!" My mom said as I played it to her a week later.

"Mom, can I ask you something?"

"Of course."

"Where is Belle?" I didn't want to bring up a tough subject with Belle around.

"Joy is taking photos of her today for practice. I think they're downstairs. You look serious, Faith. What is it?"

"Are you mad at Dad about all this? Don't you think he did the right thing by firing the drummer? I know everything is all messed up because of…because of a situation I got us into."

BEHIND THE SCENES
ON HOLLY

FULL NAME: Holly Brenique Nelson
BIRTH DATE: November 3
FAMILY MAKEUP: Dad, stepmom, two younger sisters, a younger brother
FAVORITE COLOR: Baby blue
FAVORITE FOOD: Mashed potatoes
HOBBIES: Basketball and pageants
GOALS: To maintain respect. Express her femininity. Become a pediatrician.
STRENGTHS: A born leader
WEAKNESS: Overbearing
ONE POSITIVE ABOUT THIS CHARACTER: Confident
WORD OF INFLUENCE: Power
FAVORITE PHRASE: Stand up for yourself always.

Mom looked shocked by the question and then her face softened to a look of sadness. "Oh, Faith. Yes, he did the right thing! And you did not get us into this. That man took advantage of you and the situation. He betrayed all of us."

"Then why do you seem so upset with Dad? You guys have seemed really good this year," I paused a moment before saying, "well, except back on Valentine's Day, but that was months ago. And now this stuff is happening, and it seems to be dividing the family rather than pulling us together. I can't help but feel responsible."

She took a deep breath and let out the air slowly, as if taking time to decide how to respond. "Sit down here, Faith." She patted the chair that was near the fireplace.

I sat close to her and felt the warmth of the fire and of her body as she put her arm around me. I relaxed a little.

"I haven't handled this well. I should've come to you or explained the tensions. You're so grown up in so many ways, yet you're my little girl at heart, and I want to protect you. So the idea that we did not protect you when you needed it the most is very hard to bear as a parent. When your father and I had an argument on Valentine's Day, it was because he suggested that the agency was taking too much of my time, and he was worried about you kids."

"He's busy a lot, Mom. You should have your dream too!" I said strongly.

Mom smiled slightly. "Well, you are your mother's daughter. I said the same thing to him, and that triggered the argument. I was so stubborn and prideful that I couldn't hear what he was saying. He knew you guys needed me, but I just thought your father was saying it because I wasn't as available to help him and take care of the house. I'm not here just to cook and clean. I have passions and talents too."

I didn't say it, but that sure explained why she got angry the day of Blake's party. She was mad that we were expecting her to do everything for us.

"Mom, we've gotten used to the new arrangement. And now you've hired more help. We'll find balance. Besides, Blake and Joy have learned to pitch in more."

"It has improved. Then, when Drew pursued you, your father and I both felt we were so focused on what we were doing that we missed the signs of his behavior. At first your dad got mad at me, but really his anger was at himself. Drew treated some of the background singers with disrespect, and a few of the other band members complained. Now it has snowballed **and** we didn't stop it in time to protect you. We failed you, Faith. You need to know that nothing that happened was a result of anything you did or said."

"I do know. But, Mom, the same thing you're telling me, you should be telling yourself. This

> **Value Verse**
> "We do not lose heart. Though outwardly we are wasting away, yet inwardly we are being renewed day by day."
> [2 Corinthians 4:16]

> " Other **people** can't shake you, break you, or **tear** you down. I mean, they can **if** you **let** them. "

NOVEMBER

HOLIDAYS

Election Day → November 6
Veteran's Day → November 11
Thanksgiving → November 22

HAPPY BIRTHDAY TO YOU

Nelly → November 2
Eve → November 10
Anne Hathaway → November 12

SOMETHING TO DO

Serve Thanksgiving dinner to your family or to a family in need.

Think About It

Show thanks to your family and friends. Think on all the amazing ways God has blessed you in your life.

History Lesson

In 1621, the first Thanksgiving was celebrated when the Pilgrims and the Indians worked together to live in the same place and to be at peace.

Faith's Timeline

Nov. 3rd → Holly's birthday
5th → Write another song
Thanksgiving — the grandparents are coming
Mondays, Wednesdays, Thursdays, Saturdays: cheer practice

I believe I've always been a big believer in equality. No one has ever been able to tell me I couldn't do something because I was a girl.

ANNE HATHAWAY

[blog]

>>

When I think of how much God loves me, I light up brighter than any Christmas tree.

<<

Jess | Palo Alto, CA | 12 years old | 6th Grade

---

wasn't because of something you and Dad did or didn't do. Dad was just giving the guy a chance, and Drew turned on him. What I don't understand is how the guy can be suing Dad? *He* did the bad thing."

"Well, he's shrewd, Faith. He filed the lawsuit before we could press charges for what he'd done to you. He knew he'd be in trouble, so with the lawsuit he is trying to bring down your dad's reputation and divide our family. He won't win. But we know he'll keep saying negative, nasty things because he is vengeful. Sadly, we can't stop that completely. But this will end, and he will be held responsible for his actions."

"I'd hate for him to do that to someone else, Mom," I said softly.

Mom teared up. "You are a good, wonderful, tenderhearted young woman. You really shine with God's light, Faith. I'm so in awe of you."

My mom and I shared a huge hug. Having her arms around me felt good. She'd been holding Belle a lot, and I guess in a way, I enjoyed being her baby for a moment. It was good to know she loved me, and that as a family we were going to be okay. I went upstairs to my room and relaxed on my bed until I heard my sister.

"Oh my gosh! You guys, turn on the TV!" Joy screamed.

My dad and Blake came into my room, and I turned on the television.

I couldn't believe it. There was Drew standing in front of a crowd of media.

"After further consideration, I am withdrawing my lawsuit against Jack Tyler Thomas. My opinions still stand about him, but I am following the advice of my legal counsel at this time."

A man took the mic and said, "My client will not be answering any questions at this time. We will release a statement at a later date."

My sister and I screamed and jumped up and down with big smiles. My brother and dad were high-fiving. My mom heard the screaming and was heading up the stairs at the same time we all trampled down and started telling her about the press conference. My mom's eyes welled up. She and my dad encircled all of us with their arms and we had a family hug. It was great. Dad kissed me on the forehead.

Belle, who had been sleeping through all the commotion, was walking down the stairs sluggishly, rubbing her eyes and mumbling something under her breath.

"What did you say, Belle?" I asked as she stepped off the last step and stood by me.

> **I'm learning that it is in the lowest times that God wants us to shine with His love and grace.**

"What are y'all doing?"
"Oh. We're just giving each other some love."
"Why?"
"Because that's what strong families do."
"I want some too," she said as she put both her fists down from her eyes.
"Come over here, you," my dad said as he picked her up and gave her a hug. Everyone else took turns hugging her. It felt good being part of a family that knew how to show they cared for one another.
"I think we should celebrate with ice cream!" Blake said. We all laughed.

The next day we were taking a family photo. I used to hate such things. I remember taking one not that long ago and my smile had been forced. This time my smile wasn't fake. I felt more confident than ever about God's love for me. He was helping me through so much, and yeah, life was still crazy, but it wasn't bad. That gave me reason enough to smile in a real way. I had another reason to smile. Mom told me that my braces would be coming off soon.

The next day our family picture was in the newspaper. "Thomas Family Holds Strong" was the headline. I was glad the situation turned out in our favor. My dad and mom still felt responsible for not taking care of Drew's behavior and presence in our lives earlier, but we all learned from this experience. And we were all so grateful that it hadn't been even worse. I thought back to that night in the bathroom, and the panic filled me all over again. Mom had me talk with a counselor at church, and she said that when thoughts of that night came to me, I could just keep giving them back over to God and He would change them and give me peace. I already felt some of that peace. The love of my family and of the Lord really was making me feel secure.

My dad was having a Thanksgiving concert. It was amazing how things had turned around for him. The sales with this current album exceeded all those before. His album was filled with songs about repenting and being renewed in Christ. I guess everyone could identify with redemption issues. The whole family was in his dressing room waiting for him to go sing. My mom slowly walked up to him and said to him in a sweet voice, "Jack, if you could have anything tonight, what would it be?"

We all knew the answer to that. My dad wanted a better relationship with his parents. Every time they promised to see him perform, they ended up letting him down.

I didn't fully understand all the issues between them, but overhearing conversations here and there, I got the gist of it. My grandparents had mixed feelings about my dad's success. On the one hand, they thought that fame and faith did not mix and that he had too much celebrity to be humble. On the other hand, they also felt that his success should trickle down to all his family members. He had a brother who struggled to keep a job, and they were always wanting Dad to bail him out of financial trouble. But Dad refused to keep enabling him...so the tensions just grew.

Dad hung his head low with the weight of knowing his wish might never be fulfilled. I wished I could mend the relationship for him.

My mom bent down and whispered something in his ear. My dad smiled with disbelief. He stood, looked at the door, and bowed his head. I turned around and was surprised to see my grandma and granddad crying at the door. Though I hadn't spent much time with them, they looked the same as old photos we had on our wall. My dad went up to the two of them, and they all hugged.

He cried, "Thank You, Lord!"

His mother held his face between both of her hands. "Your new album really spoke to our hearts. We've been wrong to judge you. You do so much for us, and we act like we're never grateful. You know we love you and are proud of you, don't you?"

Dad nodded, too emotional to speak.

"Your mom's right," his father said as he touched my dad's shoulder. "You're living your life for God. There are so many things you could be doing out there, but you're just trying to make a difference in this world. And success does not mean you don't have a righteous heart about your ministry. If I had not been so stubborn the past few years, you would have had a male to talk to during your hard times. I should've been available. I'm sorry, son."

My dad forgave them and it seemed like a huge cloud was lifted. We could see God working the wonder of forgiveness and healing in the family. When people make you feel worthless or cut themselves off from you, you must put it all aside and let all that hurt and anger go. God can heal you and restore relationships as if there had never been any strain.

Dad was called on to the stage, so he kissed both his parents on the cheek and walked down the curtained hallway to the performance platform.

My grandparents came over and looked at me.

"We hear you take after your father in the talent department."

"Oh, I don't know about that comparison, but I am learning that it is okay to try the things you are afraid of when it means giving your talents over to God."

Conquer Point

It's okay to be sad, but even then the Lord wants you to rejoice. He wants you to live your life to the fullest. Smile, laugh, and giggle because that is when it shows you're beaming with pride—pride in being God's daughter.

A guy with a clipboard in hand and headphones on tapped on the open door to get our attention.

"Yes?" Mom asked.

"Jack wants his folks and Faith to join him on stage."

"What?" I gasped and looked at my grandparents.

"Let's go on out there and join your dad. Maybe we can hit a note or two." Grandpa winked at me and motioned for the door. I led the way, but I still didn't understand what this was about. Why would Dad want us all on stage?

My questions were quickly answered. As soon as we were a foot away from the back curtain, two assistants handed us all microphones. Grandma and Grandpa grabbed them like pros. My hand was shaking and I was still a tad confused.

The music to "Amazing Grace" began. I couldn't believe my grandparents could sing, but they started in at the beginning of the song with my dad. There was so much I didn't know about them. I glanced around at the crowd for just a moment, and that sort of threw me. Then I closed my eyes and thought about what Dad had said. I sang to God. I sang for the people who needed encouragement. And my singing voice emerged and blended perfectly with the voices of my other family members. I felt good inside. God didn't have to bless us anymore. He gave us so much by sending His Son to die on the cross for us. Because of God's love for us, sometimes He goes above and beyond and blesses us even more. Being on stage with my family felt like one of those times for me.

Later that day, we were all at our house. My grandma came upstairs with me. She loved how my mom had decorated my room in fun colors. I passed by her, and she touched my hair.

"I remember when I was your age. I can't believe you're in high school, Faith. Your birthday is almost around the corner. I hear you gave your life to the Lord last year. How's the Christian life been?"

"It was looking a little rocky at first," I admitted.

"That's perfectly normal. I think you seem very poised in your faith."

"I have learned that He is always there for me. Just the fact that you're standing in my room after years of us not being together as a family is amazing. He keeps showing me that when He moves, His timing is perfect."

"God's blessed me with a wise, special granddaughter. How proud am I?"

We hugged, and she beamed with pride.

Prayer

Lord, I feel good, and I love feeling this way. I am getting so caught up in enjoying my relationship with You that I have no time for worrying. Thanks for showing me how to truly be joyful. I am thankful to be Your child. In Jesus' name, amen.

CHAPTER 12:

december

Shined So Bright

I'm so thankful I found out how to trust God with the drama and not live so intensely. The crown I get to wear on my head is nothing compared to the bright jewel of faith. No position or reward is as great as being in the royal family of the King.

I pray you and I can keep shining for God.

[CHAPTER 12]

Shined So Bright

I was all smiles when I came down the spiral staircase at home. The doorbell rang, and I ran to answer it. I had just come back from representing Miss Teen Nashville at a tree-lighting ceremony. I couldn't believe the end of the year was here so soon. Of course, December is my favorite month. It's the month of my birthday. But more importantly, it was when we celebrated God's gift of His Son. This year had taught me that it is this gift that gives me joy at all times.

My smile only got bigger when I opened the door and saw Hope, Kendal, and Nellie standing at my door with three different, big bouquets of roses in their hands. One was white. One was pink. And one was yellow.

"Okay, so, who died?" I asked.

"Ha-ha," Kendal said as they walked past me.

"Who's Miss Teen Nashville?" Nellie asked as she looked at my sash.

"I just had to wear it today. The girl who won has had a lot of stuff come up lately, and they keep calling me spur of the moment to fill her shoes."

"Well, you look nice," Hope said. "You look extra jazzy. We want to talk to you. Let's go up."

I thought about how important my girls were to me as I walked up behind the three of them. I couldn't make out their moods. What was going on? I didn't know they were coming. When we got into my bedroom, after they set the roses on my dresser, they all began to speak at once. When they realized that was gettin' nowhere, they let Nellie speak first.

"You've been through a lot. I know I personally gave you a hard time," she began. "Here I was telling you about how to be a Christian. 'Follow God, follow God,' I said all last year, and as soon as you accept Christ, it's like I fled from Him. What a lousy example I was, right? I wanted to give you my roses because I really am thankful that God sent you into my life."

At that point, my friend started getting choked up, so how could I remain emotionless? I stood up beside her and held her hand. I understood. She had been through a lot this year and we were still friends, even better friends, because we had stuck with one another even when we disagreed.

Nellie cleared her throat and continued. "Faith, watching you this year has shown me what a Christian walk should look like. I haven't been walking with Him. My character is horrible!"

"That's not true—"

"No, no. Don't cut me off. The three of us have been talking, and I know I've failed. You never judged me, and you helped me see that God forgives. Also, I was jealous of you being tight with these two, but now I know why you like them so much." She smiled at Hope and Kendal. They threw pillows at her from the bed, and we all laughed.

"I guess I'm just trying to say that my life is much better because you're in it. I love you, girl!" We wiped the tears from our eyes, and then we hugged.

I didn't know what Hope was going to say, but I knew I probably wouldn't be able to handle hearing her without crying.

"Okay, I get the point," I said before she could say anything.

"No, you don't. I put my roses over there on your dresser because I'm supposed to be your accountability partner. We started out one way and somehow over the course of the year, I let my anger from my home situation build and change me. I tried running away. You don't know it, but before I left that night, I was in my yard crying to God to help me. I know you prayed too, because after my dad came to get me, my stepmother and I had a long talk. Things aren't perfect by any means, but they are better. If it hadn't been for you, I wouldn't have been open to share anything with her or with my dad. My life is much better because I have a friend like you. Just watching how God allowed you to stay upbeat was empowering to me. Even my crazy sister Holly thinks you're the bomb too."

We both just smiled. She gave me a thumbs-up. I stuck my thumb up too.

"You're not going to believe what Kendal has to say," Nellie said.

"Let her tell it," Hope cut in.

"Tell me, tell me, tell me!" I shouted.

> "I **stood** up beside her and **held** her **hand**.... She had been through a lot this **year** and we were still **friends**."

"You know about me having to take algebra over. It's a good thing because now I know it, I'm building on it, and I'm excited about it. The teacher even said that if I pass this exam, I might be able to go straight into geometry second semester. That's just how well I'm doing because I'm buckling down and studying."

I opened my mouth to congratulate her when Nellie cut in. "Get to it!"

"Okay. You know how the whole God thing wasn't really for me. What you don't know is that I've been watching your life this year and I could tell that you clearly had something I was missing. You had peace and smarts and confidence, and I knew it all was because of your faith. And I didn't want to be without that. What I'm trying to say is, I gave my life to God, and I feel so complete. I was tough before and didn't think I needed anything. But the truth was...I wasn't that tough. I was pretty broken, and I needed everything

Value Verse

"You have been given fullness in Christ, who is the head over every power and authority."

[Colossians 2:10]

you have. Now I know what wholeness is, and that's why I gave you my roses, to thank you for showing me that I am loved not just by friends, but by God."

Tears were streaming down our faces. This was a good moment. God was showing me that prayer does change everything. It's not easy to get along with people when you're not perfect and they're not either, but when you truly love them, you can put aside some of the drama. When Jesus shines, His brightness will illuminate the best in your friends and, before you know it, the drama is gone. I was glad they came over. God was good. Nellie, Kendal, and Hope left soon after this, but my faith was even stronger now in God, Christ, the Holy Spirit, and the power of prayer.

Hours later my mom and I were on our way to a meeting with the people in charge of the Nashville pageant. Mom wouldn't tell me anything about what this impromptu meeting was about. When we got in the room and I saw Jillian there with her parents looking sad, I hoped she hadn't done anything wrong to lose her title. Jillian stood up and ran over to me. She gripped my shoulders and with a very serious expression, she explained the dilemma.

"We're moving. You're Miss Teen Nashville now."

I couldn't believe what she had just said to me. Yeah, I had been doing some engagements for her, but this was her crown. She'd won it fair and square, and when she did get to go out and represent, she did a great job. I couldn't take that from her.

"No, you can't move," I said aloud to her parents. "Jillian will be so great at this."

Her mom said, "Oh, Faith, what a nice girl you are. Anyone else would've been so excited to take over the crown. You're a beautiful, confident girl, but you don't have an ounce of arrogance. That is very refreshing."

"I told you she was something, Mom," Jillian said and then whispered to me, "I wanted to resent you, but you make that impossible."

I knew she meant this in the best way. "Where are you moving?"

"California!" Jillian said, absolutely thrilled. She clapped her hands and added, "Dad's going to work for a production company. He'll be doing movies, and guess what that means for me?"

"You get to audition. You'll probably be in a movie soon!"

"Exactly. That was part of our agreement as a family. If I handed the crown over to you graciously and went along with the move with a good attitude, then I can audition when we get to California. We might have to get you into some movies, Faith."

> "I've been watching *your life* this year and I could tell that you *clearly* had something I was *missing*."

"Well, if so you can contact her through my talent agency," my mom piped up, more joking than serious. But there was a certain gleam in her eye.

"That's right! I forgot you had the new agency, Mrs. Thomas. I need your card. In fact, give me several. I'll be sure Dad has a few on hand too," Jillian said.

"That is very thoughtful of you, Jillian," Mom said.

"In all honesty, Faith, you are the only person I'd feel good about giving the crown to. You're

SELF-ESTEEM GROWS

You Can Do All Things

Remember who God is. Remember who you are in Christ Jesus. Remember where there is life. If you remember those things, you will always be clear about yourself and you will always be esteemed in the kingdom of God. You are who God says you are and not who the world says you are, or even who you say you are. God loves you more than you can comprehend. There is nothing that can harm you and nothing that you cannot do when God ordains it, but it will be in His time. Don't try to rush your life. Don't rush growing up, don't rush accomplishing your goals, and don't rush God. "Being confident of this, that he who began a good work in you will carry it on to completion until the day of Christ Jesus" (Philippians 1:6).

[blog]

>>

Before I face a tough situation, I sing, "This Little Light of Mine." After that I shine because I know God is helping me glow with the light of His presence.

<<

Rhapsodi | Houston, TX | 17 years old | 12th Grade

We have no doubt that you're going to make a great Miss Teen Nashville. We're also excited to work with you so that next year you can win Miss Teen Tennessee. What do you think about that?"

"I'm just excited to be here," I said, filled with gratitude.

How neat was this? God blessed me. I didn't ask Him for more, but He gave me such a great surprise. It was so cool how God knew what I needed. I knew that learning this faith lesson now was going to be important to me in the future. I would never doubt that God understood what I needed. I would never doubt that He cared about my life even though I'm just me—I'm just one teen who makes mistakes. I vowed to myself that I was going to remain focused on Him.

It was Christmas Eve—the day before my birthday, but also the day we usually celebrated my birthday. My parents started that when I was young—so we could have my party one day and lead right into a celebration of Christ's birth the next day. It made it extra fun because it felt like one long week of family festivities. I got out of bed and walked downstairs. My family was at the dining room table, including little Belle, who was starting to

not only gorgeous on the outside, but you're good inside too. And you really shine with your faith. I sort of struggle with that, but you've been a good example to me." Jillian gracefully lifted the crown she had been holding this entire time and placed it on my head, and politely turned and went back over to her mom. Soon they left. My mom walked them out, and I was left alone with Mrs. Knight.

"How do you feel?" she asked, looking at me with pride.

"I don't know. I'm overwhelmed. I thought I was just coming here to bring back the sash, but now I get to keep it. Plus I'm taking home the crown, and Jillian's okay with it. I…I'm excited."

"We're excited for you. You've gained a lot of self-esteem, and you'll be able to identify with all those teens out there. Like you said in your answer to your question that day on the stage, you'll be able to help people understand why they are unique and lovely, just like you are.

> "We have **no doubt** that you're going to make a great **Miss Teen Nashville**."

fit in nicely with us. My dad had made pancakes. I walked up next to him.

"Happy birthday, beautiful," he said.

My mom poured freshly squeezed orange juice into her glass, and everyone else had theirs in front of them, even me. My plate was at the head of the table. After I sat down, Dad raised his glass, and everyone else followed behind him.

"Here's to Faith," he said. "We love you and are really, really proud of you. Does anyone else want to say something?"

"I love you, Faith. Thanks for being a great big sister to me. Happy birthday! Will you share your presents with me? It's okay if you get something that's just for big girls. You can give me the money," Belle sweetly exclaimed, and we all laughed.

"Belle, I promise to share anything I get."

"Faith, um, I know I'm your little brother, but … about that guy who tried to hurt you in New York … I realized that I'll always want you to be safe. You are important to me. So, I want you to have this." Blake stretched out his arm to hand me a baseball.

I smiled but he could see my confusion. I glanced down at the ball. It was autographed by a few of the New York Yankees. He and my dad had spotted it and bought it while we were all in New York. Blake had been carrying it around with him day and night ever since. I couldn't believe he was giving it to me.

"Every time you look at it, I want you to know that your little brother has got your back."

"I can't take this from you…even if it is a gift. How about you keep it for me, and when I want a reminder that we're tight like that, I'll insist on seeing it."

"Cool!" He snatched it out of my hand and looked more than a little relieved.

"What can I say? I want to be like you," Joy said. "You're Miss Teen Nashville, for goodness' sake. My sister's got it going on. Move over, Dad. She's the new star now."

That really made me feel good…not just what she said, but the fact that Joy looked up to me in any way. I used to be so jealous of her. She still was so much more together than I'd ever be, but now I could appreciate her gifts and she could appreciate mine.

"Mom's buying you that cool jacket that I helped pick out. And I didn't make a big deal about the fact that I totally wanted it for myself. That's my gift to you."

I rolled my eyes at Joy, but we smiled at each other. "Thanks, sis."

"Since she just gave away what my gift is for you, I guess I'll give you a big hug. Happy birthday, sweetie." My mom stood up and came behind me, putting her arms around me and squeezing me tight. "You, Faith, are someone we all look up to. You are caring, loving, and strong. Stay that way and the sky is the limit." She kissed me on the cheek. "Now, you had best eat your breakfast and get ready, because we have to go in…" Mom looked at her watch, "thirty minutes exactly."

"Oh, Mom. I don't want to go. I'm nervous."

"You're nervous about going shopping?" Joy asked incredulous.

Mom explained. "We are not going shopping. Your sister—I mean, Miss Teen Nashville, is going to a girls' home to give a holiday talk. It's her first official activity."

"They'll probably think I'm a total snob."

"Faith," my dad said, "this is no different than singing in front of a crowd. Think about it."

I stared at my orange juice while considering this. "I'm doing it for God and to serve Him. It isn't about me or about what people think of *me*."

Dad winked at me. "Fast learner."

When I got to the home and stood at the front of a living room with lots of couches and chairs, I looked around at the group. About 20 girls seemed either disinterested or distracted. Why did they even schedule this talk? It was clear that nobody wanted me here.

Lord, I can't do this. Then something inside of me clicked. I had gone through so much this last year, and the thing Mrs. Knight said about me not having confidence in the beginning was so true. I had changed a lot, and I had God to thank for that transformation. It also meant that I did have something important to share. Ignoring the notes I had written down as my opening line, I stood tall in front of the disinterested gathering and began to sing my song "God Wants You to Shine."

A few clusters of girls kept talking, but I kept on singing. Suddenly a girl wearing a camouflage shirt and baggy jeans stood up and waved her hands in the air.

"Wow, you have a beautiful voice," she said. "Y'all sit down and shut your mouths. Let this girl sing."

I loved that she took control. I didn't have to fight for their attention anymore. I had the floor. When I finished the song they were all focused on me. I started to talk like I would talk to Hope or Nellie or Kendal. I wanted to think of these girls as friends I just hadn't gotten to know yet.

"So we're supposed to have an open rap session just talking about whatever is going on with you guys that's got you down. I just became Miss Teen Nashville, so this experience is pretty new to me. The title doesn't mean anything except that it gives me a chance to meet other teens who are facing hard times and good times too. We're all teens. We're all going through it. We're trying to get better at this life stuff, right?"

"Yeah!" a girl shouted from the back. "But that's easy for you to say. You're standing there in perfect clothes and from a perfect family. We know you got money, girl. Look around. We don't have any of that."

"We know who your daddy is!" Another girl shouted from the back. "There's no way you can relate to us."

"That's not true. We share one parent together."

They all looked dumbfounded.

"I believe in my heavenly Father. He's my main parent."

I saw some girls look up at me, full of surprise and recognition.

"I believe that too."

"Me too."

Before I knew it, many of them were saying they loved the same God I did.

"You see…we're all in this together. We're all sisters under the same Father in heaven. And He loves us equally, even if our life circumstances are different."

"Yeah, that's what people say. But it doesn't feel like it," another girl voiced.

"Then you got to hold Him accountable for that. Take your anger and frustrations to the Lord. Let Him reveal Himself to you. Be willing to soften your heart. Okay, I know you have it

> "**I'm** doing it for God and to **serve** Him. It **isn't** about me or about what people **think** of *me*."

DECEMBER

SOMETHING TO DO
Buy a gift to bless and surprise someone at school.

THINK ABOUT IT
How has God blessed you this past year?

HOLIDAYS
Christmas → December 25
New Year's Eve → December 31

HAPPY BIRTHDAY TO YOU
Frankie J. → December 14
Christina Aguilera → December 18
JoJo → December 20
Me! → December 25
Jesus → December 25

HISTORY LESSON
Jesus' true birth date is unknown, so a date was set by the church around the old Roman Saturnalia festival (17-21 December).

Faith's Timeline

Dec. 2nd → Girlfriends realize I love them
2nd → Crowned Miss Teen Nashville
24th → Celebrating my birthday. Wow I finally feel good about me.
Mondays, Wednesdays, Thursdays, Saturdays: cheer practice

> Whatever size you are, you're beautiful. Inside and out, you should value yourself and stay away from that negativity.
> — FRANKIE J.

harder, but somebody cares enough that you have a roof over your head, and that in and of itself is a blessing. I'm Miss Teen Nashville not because of what you see on the outside, but because I'm holding my head up high on the inside. The title doesn't matter, but I think y'all agree that the attitude does."

"Amen!" one girl shouted with her hand raised.

"If I believe in my heart that God has got me covered, then what's inside of me comes shining through. We are all special."

"So you think just because we believe in God, we're suddenly sittin' pretty and lookin' beautiful? How real is that?" A girl standing against the door frame with her arms crossed looked sort of angry, but also interested. I decided to focus on the interested part.

"When you mix believing in yourself and believing in your own dreams with knowing that the Lord's with you everywhere, nothing can stop you. You'll shine in dark places. Be a light in the valley. I'm not saying life won't feel hard and be hard for a while, but it's all in what you think about your circumstances. You

> "When you **mix believing** in your own **dreams** with knowing that the **Lord's** with you everywhere, nothing can stop **you**."

guys have a network of sisters and I've only got one, and we're just getting to a point where we can enjoy each other. She used to get on my nerves."

"Like these girls get on mine," the first girl shouted out, and everyone laughed.

"Yeah, but I can tell y'all have a tight bond. That's a blessing. Whatever it is you want to be, look inside yourself and ask God to get you on the right track to make that happen. Spend time with people in that profession. If you want to be a teacher, instead of just going to school to cut up, talk to your teacher and ask her what you can do to have that same job one day. If you want to be a doctor, call some doctors and set up an interview or even see if you can volunteer in their office for a summer."

"They ain't gonna pay us no money."

"You'll be paid tomorrow. You know what I mean? Invest in your future by making decisions and taking steps that move you toward God's best for you. He has a plan and purpose for you. Hey, if you want, I'll come back and check on the progress you are making. We can keep having sessions like this." I watched as some of the girls nodded. In fact, most of them did. I decided to take a big risk. "I want you to stand up and repeat after me."

I was amazed when they all stood up, ready to follow my words.

"I am somebody special, and I have a Father in heaven who will take care of me."

The two-hour session flew by in no time. When we finished talking officially, they all rushed up to me to talk about their dreams and goals. I was so excited for them and also about this experience. I was thankful God worked through me, and I was so grateful that He had given me exactly the right words and the confidence to be here. The sad, pitiful, disrespectful girls I walked in on were gone. Standing before me were 20 girls with promise like any and every young teen girl in the world. We didn't have it all together every minute, but when we gave stuff over to God, we shined so bright!

Conquer Point

Feeling good about one's self can be difficult, however, know you are the bomb because God is the best and you are His child. Apart from Him you aren't so awesome, so stay focused on the Lord and you'll be straight.

Prayer

Dear God, I might not have the perfect body or the best teeth or the coolest clothes, but I have Your love, and that pumps me up. Help me to see me as You see me, perfectly and wonderfully made.

In Jesus' name, amen.

Scrapbooking 101

Scrapbooking is a combination of photography, design, journaling, texture, and layout. A scrapbook can become a record of your life and of the trends of the day. Scrapbooks are a way to express yourself.

To begin scrapbooking, start by sorting your photos. This can be a huge task, but once completed, it's very rewarding. Take a few photo boxes and begin to sort photos by topics: family, friends, holidays, school, vacations, etc. Then sort further by year. After you have completed this step the fun begins.

Start with one photo and pick out page colors, embellishments, borders, etc. Once you finish your first page and are pleased with your accomplishment, you will understand how this can become a hobby. One book always leads to another.

Scrapbooking supplies are limitless. Craft and hobby shows and stores are venues to discover how massive scrapping has become. Once you are into it, you can spend hours looking at all the aisles in craft stores dedicated to scrapbooking. The great thing about scrapbooking is there is no right or wrong way to do it. Each scrapbook is different and an awesome way to make your memories last a lifetime. Have fun!

SOME BASIC SUPPLIES:

Adhesives (lots to choose from, select what works best for your materials)

Photo tips to position photos on pages and makes for easy exchanges of images

Card stock and decorated papers to use as backgrounds, borders, and cutouts

Scissors—a regular pair and a pair that has a design edge to give your borders variety

Ribbons to add color, texture, and curvy lines to any page

Confetti, sparkles, paper punches with shapes to further jazz up your pages

Pens and pencils—loads of them with varied thickness and shades. Don't forget to have a few sparkle gel pens, and a decent calligraphy pen adds a lot of style to any book.

The Third Person

[JOHN 14:16–17]

We are given earthly fathers who give us an idea of God the Father, and the Bible tells us about Jesus (God the Son), but who is God the Holy Spirit?

When we are tempted to do something wrong, it's like a battle going on inside us between two parts of us. One side tries to convince us to do what is wrong, and the other urges us to make the right choice. That urge toward what is righteous and godly is the work of the Holy Spirit, guiding us and prompting us to do what is pleasing to God.

When we see someone in need or hurting and feel the desire to help, that is the Spirit of God at work in our hearts, leading us to do as Jesus did. The Holy Spirit will help us see the needs around us and, if we listen to His voice within, will give us the ability to be used by God to meet those needs. He will give us the words to say or the insight needed to find an answer. Through the power of the Holy Spirit, our lives are changed, and we can be a channel of God's blessing into the lives of others.

The Holy Spirit is the Spirit of God. His role is to bring comfort, to build us up, and to lead us to understand what is true. The Holy Spirit enables us to know God's will for our lives, to pray effectively, and to experience His power working through us. The Holy Spirit is not some ghost-like entity. He was sent to us by Jesus to guide us and enable us to live as Jesus did.

Gettin' Quiet

[PSALM 46:10]

Stand on any street corner and take time to listen. You'll hear horns blaring, music pounding, people shouting. For that matter, stand in your own home, and you'll hear the television and radio, phones ringing, people talking, computers beeping, and motors whirring. It's like a sound tsunami drowning your thoughts and suffocating your mind.

With all the clamor and activity, we have all nearly lost the ability to just spend time with ourselves in the stillness of a moment. It's important to know your own identity and discover your own thoughts. To do that, you need time away from distractions. You need to seek out a space to have alone time so you can get to know the person living inside your own skin.

Even more importantly, taking time away from the commotion of life is the best way to connect with God. He is not a distant deity, watching from afar. He is the loving Father, who wants to hear your thoughts and let you know His.

If you received an invitation to meet God Himself, would you go? Are there questions you would like to ask Him? Would you like to know more about who He is and why He acts as He does? Well, that invitation has already been sent. Throughout the pages of the Bible, God asks again and again for you to come and get to know Him. Open your Bible, your heart, and your mind, and get to know the One who created you. Find a quiet place and discover the most breathtaking sound of all, the voice of God. Being close to Him will keep you feeling great.

About the Model

NICOLE BELL is an honor roll student at a private school in Georgia. She enjoys spending time with her family and friends. Nicole loves to shop for clothes and jewelry. Her hobbies include tumbling, cheerleading, skating, dancing, and modeling. She competes on two advanced cheerleading squads at United Storm, and this is where she spends the majority of her spare time. Nicole is a flyer, and she is working on her double and standing full. She hopes to receive a cheerleading scholarship and go to a good college where she can eventually become an entrepreneur.

Nicole is an active member of the Church in the Now where she has learned many of the values she has today. Her desire is to become everything God has called her to be and to fulfill her destiny. Nicole's favorite food is steak and salad with balsamic vinaigrette dressing. She drinks lots of water! She is the oldest of three girls and lives with her dad and mom in Georgia. ✿

NICOLE'S NUGGET

Hi, everyone, it's Nicole!

This book deals with an issue I personally struggle with—self-esteem. We hear that phrase a lot, and what it means is "how much a person likes, accepts, and respects herself overall as a person." There are areas in my life that I feel confident about, and there are areas that I don't feel quite so sure of myself. If you're anything like me, I know this novelzine will help you.

I have a few friends who enjoy picking on me and telling me what to do. I sometimes walk away feeling less than good from those conversations. But God is trying to teach me to see myself as He sees me.

If you struggle with having low self-esteem, I pray you will surround yourself with good friends who build you up instead of tear you down. God has a purpose and plan for our lives. Let's walk toward that with faith in Him and in ourselves so we can shine.

About the Author

STEPHANIE PERRY MOORE is the author of the groundbreaking Payton Skky Series, the entertaining Laurel Shadrach Series, the fun-loving Carmen Browne Series and three adult Christian fiction titles. *Prime Choice*, the first book in the Perry Skky Jr. Senes is available in July 2007.

She is the co-editor for the innovative BibleZine REAL and the co-author of Sisters in Faith Bible study, to be released in September of 2007. Mrs. Moore speaks with young people across the country, showing them how they can still be cool, but do it God's way. She lives in the greater Atlanta area with her husband, Derrick, and their children.

MySpace: www.myspace.com/faiththomasseries

Xianz: www.xianz.com/faiththomas

VISIT ME IN CYBERSPACE!

SOUNDS 2 ✓ OUT

When you surround yourself with messages of God's love, you won't forget how amazingly special and beautiful you are to Him. You probably have your own music that builds you up and gets you ready for a day, but here is my playlist when I want to be reminded how to shine, shine, shine with confidence and God's grace! —Faith

In His IMAGE Mix

"All That I Can Do" + Bethany Dillon

"Courage" + Superchick

"You Get Me" + ZOEgirl

"My Answer is You" + Brian Littrell

"Mirror" + BarlowGirl

"Beautiful Stranger" + Rebecca St. James

"Overwhelm Me" + Adie Camp

"Live" + Krystal Meyers

"Incredible" + Mary Mary

"Lift Your Eyes" + Leeland

"Does Anybody Hear Her?" + Casting Crowns

"Make Me Over" + Natalie Grant

"I Am" + Nichole Nordeman

"Imagine Me" + Kirk Franklin